FROM THE
NANCY DREW FILES

THE CASE: Nancy discovers that the marriage of love and money can lead to a deadly union.

CONTACT: Charles Pierce has decided to change his will . . . and that could mean a sudden drop in his life expectancy.

SUSPECTS: Philip Pierce—*Blood is thicker than water, but Charles Pierce's son may have decided that money is more important than either.*

Jack Oliver—*Pierce's son-in-law is paying for his sins . . . and he'd like to use Pierce's money to do it.*

Eleanor Pierce—*Her brother-in-law, Charles, is her only source of income, and if he marries she fears she'll end up penniless.*

COMPLICATIONS: Nancy finds Philip Pierce's attention very hard to resist. After all, he's handsome, rich, and charming. But he's also a prime suspect in the attempted murder of his own father!

Books in The Nancy Drew Files® Series

Available from ARCHWAY Paperbacks

The Nancy Drew Files™

112

FOR LOVE OR MONEY

CAROLYN KEENE

AN ARCHWAY PAPERBACK
Published by POCKET BOOKS
New York London Toronto Sydney Tokyo Singapore

AN ARCHWAY PAPERBACK *Original*

 An Archway Paperback published by
POCKET BOOKS, a division of Simon & Schuster Inc.
1230 Avenue of the Americas, New York, NY 10020

Copyright © 1995 by Simon & Schuster Inc.
Produced by Mega-Books, Inc.

ISBN: 0-671-88203-1

First Archway Paperback printing December 1995

10 9 8 7 6 5 4 3 2 1

NANCY DREW, AN ARCHWAY PAPERBACK and colophon
are registered trademarks of Simon & Schuster Inc.

THE NANCY DREW FILES is a trademark of
Simon & Schuster Inc.

Cover photograph from "Nancy Drew" Series © 1995 Nelvana
Limited/Marathon Productions S.A. All rights reserved.

Printed in the U.S.A.

IL 6+

FOR LOVE
OR MONEY

Chapter

One

NANCY DREW, I can't believe you!" Bess Marvin's voice on the other end of the line was even more excited than usual. "How in the world did you get yourself invited?"

"Oh, just lucky, I guess," Nancy answered, checking herself out in her bedroom mirror. Her slinky, dark green dress showed off her shoulder-length reddish blond hair and big blue eyes to perfection. Too bad that her longtime boyfriend, Ned Nickerson, was off at Emerson College. He would definitely have appreciated the way she looked that evening.

"Mr. Pierce had his chauffeur hand-deliver an engraved invitation into my hot little hands," Nancy fibbed, enjoying the effect she knew she was having on Bess. Bess was one of her two oldest and best friends. The other, Bess's cousin

George Fayne, was in Florida for the week, competing in a tennis tournament.

"No way!" Bess cried. "Tell the truth, Nan. You're just saying that to torture me."

"Oh, okay," Nancy said with a laugh. "My dad did some legal work for Mr. Pierce's software company last year. I guess that's why we were invited."

"I get it," Bess said. "And the invitation said 'Carson Drew and guest,' right?" Nancy's mom had died years earlier, and Nancy often accompanied her dad to social events.

"Actually," Nancy replied, holding up the fancy, gold-trimmed invitation to examine it, "it says 'Carson and Nancy Drew.' Good old Dad, huh? He must have put in a good word for me."

"Wow!" Bess exclaimed. "A personal invite. I'm impressed, Nan. Do you know how many times I've driven by the Pierce estate and wondered what it was like inside? I'd die to get in there." There was a short pause. "I don't suppose you'd like to trade places for the night? I could tell everyone I was you—"

"Not a chance," Nancy said, grinning at her friend's wheedling tone. "Besides, I'm curious about the Pierce place myself. And even more so about Mr. Pierce and his bride-to-be."

"Oooh, me, too," Bess said. "Just think, a man in his fifties, the head of his own software company and medical research foundation, with a woman of thirty from Iceland or someplace. Sounds like the plot of a romance novel to me."

"I agree," Nancy said, cradling the phone

between her ear and her shoulder as she slipped on her shoes. "And add to that that Mr. Pierce is confined to a wheelchair because he's waiting for a heart transplant, and his fiancée, Nila Kirkedottir, is his live-in nurse and caretaker."

"I know," Bess said. "I think it's really romantic, but Brenda Carlton in her gossip column couldn't accept that two people like them could be in love. Just because he's filthy rich and she's twenty years younger doesn't automatically mean she's marrying him for his money."

"Exactly," Nancy agreed.

"I expect you to take notes tonight, Drew," Bess added. "I want the whole story, first thing tomorrow. All the juicy details—got it?"

Nancy laughed, shaking her head. "Bess, you're too much," she said. "Don't worry—I'll go right up to Mr. Pierce and demand that he tell all after I ask him to invite you to the wedding."

"Yeah, right," Bess said. "That'll be the day."

"You never know," Nancy consoled her. "You might meet them both. Stranger things have happened, after all."

Entering the Pierce mansion on her father's arm, Nancy was really impressed. Not with the opulence of the palatial estate, but rather with how homey it was. The house was festive and lively—not at all as stuffy and formal as Nancy had expected. The many wildflower arrangements, the chatter of happy guests, and the soft music played by a string quartet all contributed to the welcoming atmosphere.

Nancy and Carson gave their coats to a valet and walked through the parlor and sitting room. Here and there, Carson said hello to someone he recognized. They wove their way through the milling guests and entered the large ballroom, which had been set up with dozens of small tables along the walls. The string quartet was positioned at the far end of the room.

Nancy and her father strolled among the many guests scattered about in small clusters. Nancy overheard people talking about software and guessed that a lot of these were business associates of Pierce Software, Inc. Some of the others were probably Pierce Foundation people, she thought to herself.

"Ah, here's someone I want you to meet, Nan," Carson Drew said, leading her over to a tall, balding man of about forty. "Hello, Sam— this is my daughter, Nancy. Nan, meet Samuel Bishop, a colleague of mine who's Mr. Pierce's attorney."

"Pleased to meet you," Nancy said, shaking his hand.

"Likewise," Bishop replied. "Your father's told me a lot about you. Apparently, you're quite the detective."

Nancy nodded modestly and stole a look at her dad. He was beaming at her proudly. "I brag about Nancy every chance I get," he said. "She gives me good reason."

"Carson," Bishop said, taking his arm. "I want to ask you something about the Eastwind Bank case."

"Certainly," Carson said. "Nan, would you excuse us?"

"Sure thing," she said with a smile. "I'll go get some hors d'oeuvres."

As she made her way through the crowd, Nancy had to force herself not to eavesdrop. Being a detective had made her alert for any signs of a mystery, even in the most unlikely setting. She promised herself to resist the temptation tonight and just have a good time.

She took a mini quiche off the tray of a wandering waiter and went into the parlor in search of a glass of punch. Just as she swallowed the last bit of her quiche, the young guy at the drinks table in front of her turned around, two glasses of punch in his hand.

Nancy felt her breath catch in her chest as the young man looked right at her. He had gorgeous brown eyes, fringed by long lashes. He had strong features and a disarming, crooked grin that emphasized the deep dimples in his cheeks. His light brown hair was thick, with a shock that fell across his forehead.

"Well, hello there," he said, his voice as warm as his glance. It melted Nancy right through. "Would you like a glass of punch?"

He offered her one of his two glasses. Nancy took it, mesmerized all the while by his eyes. "Weren't you getting it for someone else?" she asked him.

"Well, I was," he admitted. "But now I've forgotten who. Your fault, Miss . . ."

"Nancy," she told him. "Nancy Drew."

5

"Nancy. My new favorite name," he said, grinning at her and brushing the shock of hair back off his forehead. It fell right back down. Nancy couldn't help smiling.

"I'm Philip. Philip Pierce," he told her. When she raised an eyebrow, he added, "Yes, Pierce of Pierce Hall. Charles Pierce is my father. Do you think there's a family resemblance?"

"I'm afraid I haven't met your dad," Nancy admitted.

"You're not alone," Philip confided, slipping an arm through hers and guiding her away from the punch bowl. "Ninety percent of the people here don't know him any better than you do. You see, he's been pretty sick the past couple of years. Never goes out anymore."

"So I've read," Nancy said.

"But you'll meet him tonight," Philip assured her. "Anyway, have a look at his portrait first." He had walked her across the room to a large, framed portrait of Charles Pierce and his bride-to-be. In it, Pierce sat in an armchair—not a wheelchair—Nancy noted. He was a nice-looking man, with strong features, like those of his son. His hair was gray and thin, and Nancy thought she could see how the artist had tried to make him look healthier than he must really be. His cheeks appeared artificially rosy somehow.

Behind him, her hands on his shoulders, stood Nila Kirkedottir, who looked younger than her thirty-three years. She had a round, pretty face with light, almost white-blond hair and ice-blue eyes.

"Well?" Philip asked her. "Do we look alike? What do you think?" Philip struck a pose mimicking that of his father's in the portrait.

Nancy laughed. "I guess so," she said. "Nila's very pretty, isn't she?"

Philip scowled. "Yes, I suppose," he said. "The old man's a sucker for blonds. My mother was blond, too, you know. Myself, I'm partial to redheads."

Nancy was surprised to feel herself blush. What was it about this guy that made him so disarming? Somehow, Philip managed to be impishly cute and drop-dead handsome all at the same time. And clearly, he was attracted to her.

Nancy warned herself not to get carried away, although she could almost hear Bess's voice saying, "Hey, Nan, he's gorgeous, he's rich, and he likes you. What more could a girl ask for?"

"Phil!" a female voice called from behind Nancy. Nancy turned to see a beautiful young woman in her early twenties, with long brown hair and wide-set green eyes, weaving through the knot of guests toward them.

"Oh, hi, Karen," Philip replied, greeting her with a kiss on the cheek. "Meet Nancy. Nancy, this is my sister, Karen. And yonder's her husband, Jack. Jack, over here," he called.

"Pleased to meet you, Nancy," Karen said. "Any friend of Phil's is a friend of mine."

"We've only just met," Nancy explained.

"Then let me be the first to warn you," Karen said, giving her brother's arm a squeeze. "He makes friends fast."

7

"Hi, everyone," Karen's husband said as he joined them. "Say, don't I know you?" he asked Nancy.

"You must have a good memory," Nancy told him, recognizing the handsome young man immediately. "I was a freshman when you were a senior at River Heights High. I had a major crush on you that year. All the girls were crazy about you, and I was as crazy as any of them."

Jack stared at her, trying to remember. He stood at least three inches taller than Philip, with even more classically perfect features. His dark hair was straight where Philip's was wavy, and his eyes were deep blue. Nancy thought he was even better looking than he had been in high school.

"Nancy," he said. "Nancy . . . Drew, right?"

"Right," she said, smiling. "I'll never forget the last-second touchdown you threw against Stockton. You were such a great quarterback. Did you keep up with football in college?"

Jack acted slightly embarrassed. "I did for a year," he said. "Then I blew out my knee."

"Oh, I'm sorry to hear that," Nancy said.

"No big deal. Actually, it was kind of lucky because that was how I met Karen. She was a candy striper at the hospital, and, well, here we are, married, four years later." He gave Karen's waist a squeeze as she stared up into his eyes, clearly in love with her handsome husband.

"Nancy here was just admiring Dad's portrait," Philip told them. "She thinks Nila's pretty."

8

"Pretty? I guess you could call her that," Jack said, scowling. "It's hard to think of her that way, once you know her, though."

"Really?" Nancy asked.

"We call her the ice queen," Philip confided. "When you meet her, you'll know why."

"He means," Karen added, "that one look from her can freeze you solid." They all laughed, but Nancy felt uncomfortable and didn't join in. After all, she was at Nila's engagement party. It would have been wrong, she felt, to have a laugh at the woman's expense.

"She sure melted Dad's heart," Philip said mockingly. Nancy was taken aback by the bitterness in his voice.

"Let's hope she doesn't melt it right into the grave," Karen said, her expression darkening.

Nancy didn't know what to say, so she didn't say anything. She smiled weakly and suddenly she couldn't wait to get away from them, or at least, from this conversation.

"Er, Ms. Drew?" Nancy turned to see a butler standing behind her.

"Yes, that's me," Nancy said. Perfect timing, Nancy couldn't help thinking.

"Mr. Pierce would like to see you in his study, if you don't mind," the butler said.

Nancy's three companions looked at her in surprise. "I thought you'd never met Dad," Philip commented, faintly amused.

"I haven't," Nancy told him. "But I guess I'm about to. Excuse me."

She followed the butler out of the room,

strangely relieved and curious. Why would Mr. Pierce want to see her? The butler led the way past the large double staircase, through a huge oak door, and down a carpeted hallway to another door, where he stopped to knock.

"Come in," a weak, gravelly voice called out.

The butler opened the door. "Ms. Nancy Drew," he announced, then closed the door, leaving Nancy alone with Charles Pierce.

Mr. Pierce sat facing her in a wheelchair, much older and feebler than he appeared in his portrait. She wondered if the artist had flattered Nila as well.

"I understand from Mr. Bishop, my lawyer, that you're quite a detective," Pierce began, indicating a chair for her to sit on.

"I've solved a number of cases," Nancy said, taking the seat.

"Yes. That's why I invited you tonight," Pierce said, wheeling himself closer to her. "I'm not a man to mince words, young lady, I want to engage your services."

He studied Nancy closely, as if trying to determine whether she was up to the job he had in mind for her.

"I'd like you to investigate my family. You see, Ms. Drew," he said, his eyes boring into hers. "I'm afraid one of them may be plotting to kill my fiancée."

Chapter

Two

A HEAVY SILENCE filled the room as Nancy took in what Charles Pierce had just told her. The ticking of the grandfather clock behind Pierce's gigantic mahogany desk seemed unnaturally loud. The party going on down the hall might as well have been a million miles away.

"Are you sure about this, Mr. Pierce?" Nancy asked carefully. "I don't mean to doubt you, but normally, I don't take on an investigation unless there's been a crime, or at least evidence that one is going to happen."

Pierce nodded approvingly. "I see that you're a young lady with a good head on your shoulders," he said, fishing in his desk drawer for something. A moment later he produced a sheet of wrinkled paper, which he handed across to Nancy. "Have a look at that and then tell me what you think. It was shoved under Nila's bedroom door last week."

There was a message on the piece of paper, made from letters cut out of magazines. It read, "If you want to live, leave this place now and don't come back."

Nancy folded the paper, put it down on the desk, and gazed at Pierce. "Have you shown this to the police?" she asked.

"Ah, I thought you'd ask me that," Pierce said. "I considered showing it to them, but decided against it. The publicity, you know. A man in my position has a reputation to protect. Not just for myself, but for my entire family."

"Since you want me to investigate your family," Nancy said, "I gather you're not exactly thrilled with them at the moment."

"You've got that right," Pierce said, scowling.

"But I met your children just now, and they didn't express any resentment. At least, not toward you . . ." Nancy's voice trailed off as she remembered the way Philip, Karen, and Jack had joked so bitterly about Nila.

"Well, the children and I were estranged for a while after Dierdre's death," Pierce said. "In fact, it was only after my first heart attack that they began coming around to see me again. I suppose they felt guilty for ignoring me all those years. Or else . . ." His voice faltered for a moment. "Or else, they simply smelled money and came running to make sure they got their share."

"Do they spend a lot of time with you now?" Nancy asked.

Pierce let out a short, unhappy bark of a laugh. "It's all I can do to fight them off," he said. "Or rather, all Nila can do. I'm too weak lately to fight off anything."

"So Nila was already on the scene when they showed up?" Nancy asked.

"Yes," Pierce said, smiling wistfully at the memory of it. "She was my nurse when I first got home from the hospital. An angel. By the time I was back on my feet again, we were head over heels in love."

"Your children don't like Nila, do they?" Nancy asked.

"They certainly resent her influence over me. They think she's only after me for my money. But I assure you, Nancy—may I call you Nancy?"

"If we're going to work together, you'd better," Nancy said with a smile.

"So you'll take on the investigation?" he asked.

"I'm thinking about it," Nancy said. "Tell me more."

"Well, let me say right now that what Nila and I have is the real thing. If I were a pauper, Nila would still be crazy about me. I can't explain it to you, but there it is. Love is sometimes like that."

Nancy frowned. It certainly would be hard to explain why a woman with Nila's youth and good looks would go for a man of Pierce's age and health. Nancy wanted to believe what he was telling her, but she had to wonder if Nila's motives were as pure as he was painting them.

13

"Tell me, Mr. Pierce," Nancy said, "what are the terms of your present will?"

"Well, that's partly why I called you," he replied. "My current will splits my estate five ways. One third goes to my foundation for cardiac research. One third goes to Nila. And the last third is split evenly among Philip, Karen, and my sister-in-law, Eleanor. She and her daughter, Cecilia, are my only other living relatives."

"I haven't met Eleanor," Nancy said. "Is she here tonight?"

"Oh, yes," Pierce answered. "She and Cecilia live right here, upstairs in the west wing on the second floor. They moved in just after my brother died. That would be about three years ago. It was supposed to be a temporary arrangement, but it's dragged on into something more permanent, I'm afraid. I know it would be better for them to get out on their own. Nila's always telling me so. But I just can't bring myself to push them out of the nest."

"How did your brother die?" Nancy wondered.

"Awful. Plane crash," Pierce told her. "Poor Edwin . . . He was just about to file for bankruptcy protection, but because he died before he could file, his creditors attached his entire estate, leaving Eleanor and Cecilia penniless. So, of course, I took them in. Poor Eleanor would have gone under otherwise. She's got absolutely no life skills at all because she married before she finished school and has always been pampered.

She's such a timid creature. And Cecilia seems to be taking after her mother, I'm afraid."

"I see," Nancy said, taking out a notepad and jotting down some of what Pierce was telling her. "And now you're thinking of changing your will."

Pierce reddened a little, and Nancy could see that the thought of it was upsetting him. "Yes," he said. "The closer Nila and I have gotten, the more my family resents her. They think she's got me wrapped around her little finger, and that they're in danger of losing their inheritances. Well, the fact is that I would never have cut them off—but now, with this letter, I just don't know. . . ."

"Remember, sir, we don't know who wrote the letter," Nancy reminded him. "Now, Nila—"

"If you're suggesting that Nila wrote it herself, to turn me against my family, you're dead wrong," Pierce shouted, his face becoming purple with rage. Nancy was startled by his vehemence. Then all the color drained from his cheeks, and his eyes widened with fear. He fumbled in his pocket for a pill, put it between his teeth, and bit down on it. Moments later his color returned to normal.

"Are you all right, Mr. Pierce?" Nancy asked. "Do you want me to get a doctor?"

"No, no," he assured her. "I'm all right now. These nitroglycerine pills, along with the medications I take at night, keep me alive."

Satisfied that Mr. Pierce was fine, Nancy went

on with her questions. "What made you say that?" she asked. "About Nila forging the letter, I mean."

"It's what my daughter, Karen, said," Pierce told her. "I showed her the letter, and she said Nila probably wrote it herself. The nerve!"

Nancy wondered if Karen might have been right.

"At any rate," Pierce continued, "I'm now considering cutting Philip and Karen out of my will. Eleanor, too. I've done a lot for her, but it's not doing her or her daughter any good being so dependent on me. Nila's right. They have to learn to stand on their own. At any rate, I'm considering cutting them all off and leaving everything to Nila. I wrote up a draft of just such a will after Nila brought me the letter. It's sitting in my desk drawer there, and depending on the outcome of your inquiry, I'll either have Bishop draw it up formally or I won't."

"Tell me about Philip and Karen," Nancy pressed. "You don't seem happy with how they've turned out."

Pierce nodded slowly. "Philip's a spender," he said. "Went through his inheritance from his mother in just two years. I don't know what he does in his spare time, but it certainly costs a lot. He and Karen sold their mother's house three years ago, when Karen married Jack. Karen moved in with her new husband, and Philip took an apartment. Then, when his money ran out, Philip asked if he could stay here. I let him, of course. He may have no money sense, but he is my son.

"I hired him to work at my software company, but that didn't pan out. Since then I've been giving him a substantial allowance so that he can get out and find work somewhere else. But he's gone and squandered that money, too. Last month I told him I'd stop the allowance altogether if he didn't shape up."

"And Karen?" Nancy asked. "What about her? And Jack?"

Pierce's expression showed his disgust. "She's all right," he said. "It's that husband of hers. Talk about marrying people for their money. Jack's a gold-digger if ever there was one. He's got one scheme after the other for me to invest in. But after his first one, a restaurant, I won't trust him with a dime."

"Restaurant?"

"It was a sports theme place. Jack had been a high school football hero, and his restaurant should have had a chance, but it didn't last more than two or three months. It didn't make sense. Karen always said they were doing well, but I'm convinced Jack was up to something. Exactly what I don't know."

Just then the grandfather clock struck eight. Pierce wheeled his chair toward the door. "If you'll forgive me, I've got to go upstairs to have Nila give me my medication before I join my guests. There are so many pills it's hard for me to keep track, so Nila always does it. At any rate, I'd better get up there. It's been rude of me to make everyone wait so long to see the guests of honor."

Nancy wheeled him out into the hall and onto his little elevator.

"You don't have to give me an answer now," he told Nancy. "But if you're going to take the case, it would help if you got started as soon as possible. As you can see, time may be of the essence. As far as I'm concerned, it's a matter of life and death." The elevator door closed behind him.

Nancy stood in the quiet, gray-carpeted hall, thinking about all she'd learned. Bess would be thrilled with all the Pierce family dirt, but was there any real danger lurking here at the estate? Or was Charles Pierce making a mountain out of a molehill?

Just then, as if in answer to Nancy's silent question, a bloodcurdling scream pierced the quiet of the hallway. Nancy raced toward the sound, and then froze as she rounded a corner of the hall.

A woman who Nancy guessed was in her late forties was kneeling over the prone body of a blond-haired beauty whom Nancy recognized as Nila Kirkedottir. A dark red stain was spread out around Nila, soiling the gray carpet.

"She's dead!" the kneeling woman screamed. "Oh, my heavens, she's dead!"

Chapter

Three

Nancy quickly knelt down and grabbed Nila's limp arm to feel for a pulse. Fortunately, there was one, although it seemed a little erratic. Nancy touched the damp red stain on the carpet and was relieved that it wasn't blood but whatever had been in Nila's glass instead, which lay on the carpet next to her.

"What happened?" Nancy asked the hysterical, sobbing woman, who was also holding an empty glass. "Don't worry, she's not dead."

"Are you sure?" the woman asked, grabbing Nancy's arm with her free hand.

"Yes, I'm sure," Nancy said. "Now, please, it's important."

"I was just walking down the hall, when I saw her lying here. I swear I didn't do anything! Please—you've got to believe me!"

Nancy thought it odd that the woman would

be protesting her innocence, when as far as she could tell, Nila had simply fainted.

Just then Nila began to stir. She groaned, her face contorted in agony. "My stomach . . ." she said. "Oh, it hurts so much."

At that moment an elderly woman dressed in a uniform rounded the corner of the hallway. "Miss Nila!" the woman cried. "Oh, Miss Eleanor, is she all right?"

"You'd better see if there's a doctor at the party," Nancy told her. "And while you're at it, call an ambulance. I don't know what's wrong with Nila, but we'd better not take any chances."

The servant went off to carry out Nancy's instructions. Nancy glanced briefly at Eleanor, who was sobbing more softly now, then turned her attention to Nila, who was still in considerable pain.

"Can you tell me what happened?" Nancy asked, cradling Nila's head in her arms.

"The cranberry juice . . ." Nila moaned. "I was fine until I drank it, then suddenly—ooohhh! The pain. It's horrible. Help me, please!"

"You think there was something wrong with your juice?" Nancy asked.

Nila nodded, wincing. "It tasted horrible—bitter. Suddenly my stomach hurt so badly . . . like a knife going into it. I think I fainted from the pain. Please—please help me. Someone's—trying to kill me. . . ."

By this time a crowd of worried guests had begun gathering in the hallway. One woman, whom Nancy had noticed earlier, said, "I'm a doctor. Let me see her." She knelt down beside Nancy and took Nila's pulse.

The guests murmured in anxious tones at the ominous turn the party had suddenly taken.

Nancy grabbed the empty glass off the carpet and smelled it. "Cranberry juice," she murmured. Feeling something wet on her leg, she realized to her annoyance that she'd gotten some of the spilled juice on the hem of her brand-new dress.

This was no time to worry about whether the stain would come out, though. Sirens grew louder. The ambulance was on its way. Now Nancy could hear Pierce's voice from behind the crowd, shouting, "Get out of my way! Let me see her."

The crowd parted, and Pierce, his face ashen, wheeled close to where Nila lay. "Is she all right?" he asked the doctor.

"Her vital signs seem to be stable, as far as I can tell," she told him. "Probably food poisoning of some kind. But let's see what they say at the hospital."

"I—I thought she was dead," Eleanor Pierce said in a breathy voice. A girl about Nancy's age, with short brown hair and intense gray eyes, came up and embraced the shaken older woman. Nancy figured that this must be her daughter, Cecilia.

"What happened, Mother?" the young woman asked, stealing a glance at Nila, who was still moaning in pain.

"She—she must have fainted, dear," Eleanor

21

said, stroking her daughter's hair. "I'm sure Nila will be fine. There's nothing to worry about."

Just then two paramedics ran in, pushing a gurney. They were followed by the elderly servant.

"What's up?" one paramedic asked the doctor as he checked Nila's vital signs.

"Stomach distress," the doctor said.

"Okay, let's get her out to the ambulance," said the other paramedic.

The paramedics lifted Nila onto the gurney and rolled her away. The crowd of guests dispersed and headed back to the front rooms, speaking in hushed tones. They all seemed uncertain about how to react to what had happened.

Nancy, Pierce, Eleanor, and Cecilia remained behind. Jack, Karen, and Philip were nowhere to be seen. Nancy wondered why. With all the commotion, she would have thought they'd be curious to find out what was going on.

Cecilia took in the dark red stain on the carpet. "Oh!" she gasped. "Is it blood?" She bent down to study it more closely.

"No," Eleanor told her. "It's only cranberry juice, dear. Please, don't upset yourself. Everything will be fine. I'm sure Nila's all right."

The invalid millionaire gazed up at Nancy, an intent expression on his face. "Now what do you say, Ms. Drew?" he asked. "Will you agree to my request?"

Nancy nodded slowly. "You've got yourself a deal, Mr. Pierce," she said grimly.

"I don't understand," Eleanor said, glancing from Pierce to Nancy and back to Pierce again.

"This young lady is a detective," Pierce blurted out before Nancy could stop him. "I've engaged her to look into things around here. You remember that letter I showed you, Eleanor. And now this . . ."

Eleanor suddenly went white. With a nod toward Cecilia, who was kneeling a few feet away, staring at the stain on the carpet, Pierce added, "Now, keep this under your hat, Eleanor—understand? I don't want my children to know."

"Of course not, Charles. I understand completely."

Cecilia got to her feet and took her mother's hand. "What's this all about?" she asked, glancing suspiciously at Nancy.

"Nothing, dear," Eleanor fibbed. "Just some financial work this young lady will be doing for Uncle Charles. She may need to ask us a few questions. Isn't that right, Charles?"

Pierce scowled, his mind on other things. "I'm going to have Hastings drive me to the hospital," he announced. "Nila may need me."

"Are you sure that's wise, Charles?" Eleanor asked him. "After all, your health . . ."

"My health doesn't mean a thing to me without Nila," he told her curtly.

"But—but what about your guests?" Eleanor asked anxiously. "What shall I tell them?"

"Tell them to go home," he barked, wheeling

himself past her and down the hallway. "This party is over!"

He left the three of them standing and staring after him. Eleanor suddenly realized she was holding an empty glass and looked around for a place to put it down. "I'd better go tell the butler to make an announcement," she said.

Cecilia shot Nancy a nervous glance. "I'll come with you, Mother," she said, and they walked off together.

Nancy stood alone in the corridor, silent now after all the commotion. She could have strangled Pierce for telling Eleanor she was a detective. How could he expect her to investigate if everyone knew what she was up to?

She sniffed Nila's glass, which she'd been holding all this time. Cranberry juice. No suspicious smell, but then, it could have worn off by now. Or whatever was added to the drink could have done the job without leaving a telltale smell.

Carson Drew came walking down the hallway toward her, wearing his coat. He had hers over one arm. "I heard what happened," he said. "We weren't allowed back here until now. Is Nila all right?"

"They've taken her to the hospital," Nancy told him.

"The butler announced that the party's been called off because of Nila's severe indigestion, he said."

Nancy frowned. "Maybe," she said.

"What have you got there, Nan?" he asked,

noticing the glass in her hand. "You're holding it like it's evidence."

"It might be, Dad. It turns out Mr. Pierce invited me here so he could ask me to investigate his family. He thinks one of them might be trying to kill his fiancée."

"And what do you think, Nan?" Carson asked.

Nancy scowled. "I'm not sure yet."

"Well, here's your coat and bag. Shall we go? Or do you need to do some investigating first?"

"I'll be ready in a minute, Dad. I just want to say goodbye to some people I met."

"Okay. I'll meet you at the front door in five minutes," Carson said, leaving her there.

Nancy donned her coat and dropped the glass into her bag. Then she headed back toward the ballroom, passing through the front parlor to get there. Guests were streaming by her, heading toward the front door.

"Nancy!" She turned quickly at the sound of Philip's voice. He came up beside her, with an adorable pout on his face. "You're not leaving, are you? We've barely gotten acquainted."

Knowing she needed to get to know Philip Pierce and his family better, Nancy said, "Well, I suppose we could get together some other time. . . ."

"Excellent idea," he said, his eyes glittering. In spite of what she'd just witnessed, and all she'd heard about Philip from his father, Nancy found herself melting at his glance. It wasn't just business, she knew. She wanted to see Philip Pierce again.

"You don't have to go right away, do you?" he asked, leading her into the ballroom, away from the front door. "I'm dying to hear what Dad said to you. And what happened to Nila? I was out on the verandah in back when I heard the sirens. There was such a crowd in the hallway that I gave up trying to push through. Is she all right?"

"I think she'll be fine," Nancy said. "She fainted but had bad stomach pains when she came to. She thought she'd been poisoned."

To Nancy's surprise, Philip laughed. "Ha! That's a good one," he said. "Did she tell you about the threatening letter she got, too?"

"No," Nancy said truthfully, not volunteering that Mr. Pierce had told her. "What letter?"

"Dad showed us a letter Nila claims someone sent her, threatening her life unless she left here forever. So I guess this last bit is part of the same charade."

"Charade?" Nancy's eyes widened.

Philip stared at her, amused. "Well, yes, of course. Don't you get it? It's all part of Nila's plan to turn Dad against us."

"How can you be so sure of that?" Nancy asked.

"If you knew Nila, and what a manipulator she is, you'd understand," he told her. "The way she suckered the old man in, making him fall in love with her when he was sick and vulnerable. This is just a scheme of hers to make Dad cut his family out of his will and give everything to her instead."

Nancy's expression must have seemed skeptical because Philip went on to say, "Just you wait. I'll lay you odds that when the hospital report comes back, it'll say there was nothing wrong with Nila. And if there was, she did it to herself. Remember, she's a trained nurse. She'd know just how much of whatever to take."

Nancy had to admit that Philip had a point. It was a definite possibility that Nila was manipulating the situation. But Nancy would know more after she'd had the glass analyzed. Her friend Ernie Watkins worked at the police lab, and he owed her a favor. She'd get him to run an analysis on the residue in the glass.

Just then Jack and Karen came into the parlor. "So much for the happy engagement party," Jack commented. "Hello, Nancy. How did it go with Charles?"

"Yes, what did he want to talk to you about?" Karen asked, clearly curious.

"We never really got into it," Nancy lied. "Eleanor found Nila lying on the floor and screamed. Next thing we knew, we were in the middle of this whole chaotic scene. I guess I'll have to come back some other time to talk to your father about what he wanted to say."

"Great idea," Philip said. "Then I'll get to see you again real soon. And while we're on the subject, are you busy tomorrow night? I'm in the mood to have some fun. And I know I'll have a lot more fun if you're there to share it with me. What do you say?"

Nancy grinned back at him. "I say yes," she said.

"That's my brother," Karen said with a laugh. "A real fast mover."

"Nice meeting you all," Nancy said. "I guess I'll be seeing you again soon. And, Philip, here's my number," she added, scribbling it down on a piece of paper. "Call me tomorrow to let me know when and where, okay?"

"You can count on it," he told her, squeezing her hand and peering deeply into her eyes before letting her go.

Nancy rejoined her dad at the front door, and asked him to wait outside for her a minute. Handing him her coat and bag, she ran back toward Pierce's study. She'd forgotten to take the threatening note with her and wanted to retrieve it.

After she jogged down the carpeted hallway, she was surprised to see that the door to the study was half open. Funny, she thought. She was sure she'd closed it when she'd wheeled Mr. Pierce out of there.

Nancy tiptoed up to the door and gently pushed it open. In the dark room, she saw something or someone move.

It was the shadowy figure of a man—and he was rummaging around in Charles Pierce's desk!

Chapter

Four

NANCY REACHED OUT with her right hand and swept it up and down the wall, hoping to find the light switch and flip it on. It took her two tries to locate it, and by the time the room was lit up, the man was already standing at the open French doors, ready to leave. She made a run at him, but he pushed the desk chair in her path, and by the time she made it to the doors, he had disappeared into the darkness of the garden.

Nancy briefly thought of going after him. But in her dress and heels, she knew she'd never catch him. And running barefoot in the darkness was not a good idea, she knew. One injury could put her out of action for weeks.

Instead, she turned and looked at the contents of the single desk drawer that had been yanked open. Pierce's check ledger was inside, as was a schedule book, paper-clipped open to the page for the current week. In the box for that day's date was a notation in Pierce's spindly handwriting: "N. DREW, INVESTIGATOR."

Had the intruder seen the notation? Nancy wondered. He must have had a flashlight, she reasoned, and turned it off when he heard her approaching. Whatever he was searching for, he would have needed light to find it.

Nancy decided not to worry about the notation in Pierce's datebook. After all, Pierce had already blown her cover by mentioning her occupation in front of his sister-in-law, Eleanor, and his niece, Cecilia. Nancy would have to proceed as if everyone concerned knew about her.

She continued looking at the contents of the drawer. There was a confidential report from a supervisor at Pierce's software company, regarding Jack's performance on his current job. Apparently, Pierce had given his son-in-law a job at the firm when Jack's restaurant went under. But Jack was obviously not working out as an employee. The report described him as lazy and incompetent, unable or unwilling to perform any of the various jobs to which he'd been assigned. Nancy filed the information away in her mental databank for future reference and went on with her search.

The checkbook ledger contained nothing revealing. But when Nancy picked it up, she found a large wad of hundred-dollar bills underneath. Had the intruder seen the cash? Probably not. Even if money wasn't what he'd come for, such a large amount would not have been easy to resist.

What alarmed Nancy was not what was in the desk drawer, but what she realized was missing—the draft of Pierce's new will. There was no sign of it.

Bingo, Nancy thought, taking the threatening note she'd left on the desktop and retreating from the room after giving it a final once-over. Someone had wanted to get hold of that will, and that someone had succeeded. As she walked down the hallway to the front of the mansion, Nancy wondered about the intruder—who he was and what connection he had to the Pierce family. She knew he hadn't been either Jack or Philip. Nor had she spotted him among the guests that evening. She hadn't gotten a good look at his face, but she did notice he had long, dark hair and a compact, muscular build, and had been wearing jeans, sneakers, and a dark leather jacket.

Above all, she wondered why he, or whoever had sent him, wanted to see the draft of Pierce's new will and what would be done with the information.

"Got what you needed?" Carson asked her when she emerged from the house.

"That, and more," Nancy replied as they headed for his car.

The telephone woke Nancy at eight the next morning. "Tell me everything," Bess's voice bubbled over the line. "Don't spare a single juicy detail."

"Bess, I'm still half asleep," Nancy said, yawning and stretching. "Why don't you come over? I've got an errand to run, but I should be back by ten or so."

"I'll be there," Bess said, and hung up.

Nancy got dressed, wolfed down a bowl of cereal, and grabbed her bag, which still contained the cranberry juice glass she'd picked up from the floor of the Pierce mansion. She ran it over to police headquarters and gave it to Ernie Watkins, who promised to check out the contents and call her with the results.

She got home at a quarter to ten. Bess, impatient as always, was already in Nancy's kitchen waiting for her, a cheese sandwich in her hand. "Mmmph," she greeted Nancy with a full mouth. "I've got to quit stuffing my face, but I can't seem to help myself. Curiosity makes me hungry."

Nancy laughed, shaking her head. Bess had been trying to lose those last pesky five or ten pounds for years. Not that she was really overweight. With her pretty, blond, blue-eyed looks, Bess's extra pounds were more of a mental problem than a physical one.

Nancy plopped down on the chair next to her friend. "You would have loved it, Bess," she began, and then proceeded to tell her all the events of the night before.

"Wow," Bess said after Nancy related her conversation with Pierce. "So you're going to investigate? Fantastic! I could help you, Nan. We could check out every room of the place, and you could introduce me to Philip—he sounds so cute. Hey, maybe he's got a rich, handsome friend?"

"Whoa, hold on, Bess." Nancy held up a hand to stop her, laughing. "Sure, you can help me, but take it easy, okay? This is serious business. It may even be life and death."

"So you really think someone tried to kill Nila?" Bess asked.

"I'm not sure," Nancy told her. "Things don't really add up. Most of the contents of the glass were spilled on the carpet—there was a huge puddle of the stuff—which means she didn't drink very much of it. Then there's the letter. And most of all, the fact that somebody broke into Pierce's desk later that night and stole the draft copy of his new will. If Nila was faking the whole thing, how does that fit in?"

"It doesn't," Bess agreed. "Unless it was a total coincidence, and one thing has nothing to do with the other."

"Could be," Nancy said skeptically. "But until I hear from Ernie Watkins at the police lab, I have to assume someone doctored that cranberry juice. Anyway, we should know before too long."

At that very moment, the telephone rang. Bess, who considered herself family, not company, leaped up and answered. "Drew residence," she said. "No, this is her friend Bess. Who's this?" Her eyes widened slowly as she covered the mouthpiece. "It's the police lab," she whispered to Nancy. "For you."

33

"That was fast," Nancy commented, getting up and taking the phone from Bess. "Hi, Ernie," she said. "Finished already?"

"Yup," he told her. "And I'm sure you'll be glad to hear what I found in the glass."

"Yes?"

"Cranberry juice."

"And . . . ?"

"That's it. Cranberry juice, and nothing else."

"Ernie, are you sure?" Nancy asked, putting a hand to her forehead.

"Positive," he said. "No poison, no nothing. Your 'victim' must have faked the whole thing!"

Chapter

Five

N ANCY HUNG UP THE PHONE, perplexed. "It looks like Nila faked the poisoning incident," she told Bess. "I guess this means she could have faked the threatening letter, too."

"So are you still going to investigate?" Bess asked tentatively.

"You'd better believe it," Nancy assured her. "Mr. Pierce wanted me to check out his family. If his fiancée is trying to cheat them out of their inheritance, I'm going to find out and tell Mr. Pierce about it."

"Excellent!" Bess said enthusiastically. "So I still get to go over there with you?"

"Sure," Nancy told her. "There's a lot to check out, and I could use your help investigating. But not this time, okay?"

"What?" Bess asked, startled by Nancy's bolting out of her chair. "Hey, where are you going? Don't go without me."

"Have to this time, Bess," Nancy said at the door. "I can't just bring you with me without telling Pierce about you first. Give me a chance to straighten things out and get organized. Don't worry, you'll get to see the place."

"And meet your new romance," Bess reminded her.

"Quit it, Bess," Nancy said. "Philip Pierce is simply one of the subjects of my investigation, okay?"

"Whatever you say, Drew," Bess said dryly. "But you can't fool me. I heard the catch in your voice when you described him. Just remember to ask if he's got a friend."

Bess popped the rest of the cheese sandwich into her mouth and winked at Nancy. "When opportunity knocks, Nan," she said, "you've got to answer the door."

When she arrived at the Pierce mansion, Nancy decided that instead of going straight to the front door and ringing the bell, she'd walk around to the rear of the house. She wanted to see the French doors the intruder had used. Perhaps he'd left a footprint or some other clue to his identity.

But as she rounded the corner of the house, she saw something that aroused her curiosity even more. Pierce's sister-in-law, Eleanor, was moving toward a row of garbage cans, holding a bag in her hands and looking around furtively as if she were afraid someone would spot her.

Nancy watched as Eleanor lifted the lid of one of the cans, dropped the bag inside, and hurriedly slammed the lid back down. With another furtive glance around, Eleanor headed back to the house.

When the woman was safely inside, Nancy went over to the trash can and opened the lid. The bag inside had a large skull on it. "'Rat poison,'" Nancy read out loud. "'Keep out of reach of children and pets.'"

Nancy knew that rat poison might reasonably be kept around the mansion, but she had to wonder why Eleanor was so secretive about throwing it away.

Just then Cecilia came around the corner of the house. "Oh. Hello," she said, giving Nan a quick smile.

"Hello, Cecilia," Nancy said.

"Did you leave something behind last night? Is that why you're here?" Cecilia asked. She had to have heard Pierce telling Eleanor the night before that Nancy was a detective, but she wasn't letting on that she knew.

"Er, no," Nancy said. "Actually, I came by to see how Nila was doing. Has she recovered from her sudden illness last night."

"She's all right," Cecilia said, frowning. "They brought her back around midnight. She looked just fine to me."

"Is she feeling better then?" Nancy asked.

"She seems to be her usual self again. I heard her shouting at the servants this morning."

"Oh," Nancy said. "Does she do that often?"

"All the time," Cecilia said. "It's awful the way she treats them. She thinks everyone's out to get her or something. I mean, really." Cecilia rolled her eyes in obvious disgust.

"Tell me," Nancy said. "I get the impression Nila isn't very popular around here. Am I wrong?"

The corner of Cecilia's mouth turned upward in a sly smile. "Philip and Karen can't stand her. And Jack—well, I think he'd like to strangle her sometimes." She giggled at the thought.

"Do you think she's your enemy, too?" Nancy asked boldly.

"Me?" Cecilia repeated. Nancy thought the girl was startled by the question. "No, of course not."

"Then you and Nila are on good terms?" Nancy pressed.

"I—I . . . well . . ."

"What about your mother?" Nancy pressed. "Does she feel threatened by Nila, too?"

Cecilia's expression suddenly hardened. "What business is it of yours?" she demanded. "Who told you to come snooping around here anyway?"

"There's no reason to get upset," Nancy said, backing off. "I was just curious, that's all. . . ."

Cecilia shot her a hostile glance, then turned and went inside without another word.

Nancy stared after her, disturbed. Eleanor's

and Cecilia's odd behavior made her wonder if they were simply two unfortunate relatives, or if they, Eleanor in particular, had something to hide. . . .

Nancy went around to the front door and rang the bell. The butler informed her that Mr. Pierce was not feeling well and was not receiving visitors. Nancy asked if she could see Nila, and the butler directed her to a small sofa in the front parlor. He went off to tell Nila she had a visitor.

While Nancy waited, she thought about what had just happened. Rat poison contained strychnine, she knew. And strychnine would have been consistent with Nila's symptoms of the night before—if she'd only swallowed a little bit of it. Judging by all the cranberry juice on the floor, she'd only taken a sip or two.

On the other hand, the glass had been found to be clean. No strychnine at all. So why was Eleanor skulking around, trying to get rid of rat poison without anyone's seeing her? It didn't make sense.

The butler returned. "Miss Nila will see you in a few minutes, if you care to wait," he said with a little bow. "She's just finishing breakfast."

Nancy noted the fact that Nila was feeling well enough to eat, after her ordeal. "Thank you," she said. "Tell me, how is she doing today?"

"Oh, much better, miss," the butler told her. "She seems to be just fine. Which is more than can be said for Mr. Pierce. He couldn't even get out of bed this morning."

"Really?" Nancy asked. "I suppose his children are at his bedside—"

39

"Er, no, miss," the butler told her. "Master Philip is having a game of tennis with Miss Karen, I believe." He looked out the window disapprovingly.

"I take it you think they ought to be more attentive to their father?" Nancy prodded him.

"I wouldn't like to say, miss," he told her. "But it does seem to me—"

"Jarvis!" Nila Kirkedottir stood in the parlor doorway, wearing a gold-brocaded robe, her ice-blue eyes flashing.

"Madam—"

"Chatting with the guests?" Nila asked. "Get out of here this instant." The butler bowed and walked off.

"I can't stand it when servants gossip with visitors," Nila said, sitting down in an armchair. "He knows very well what his job is."

"He really didn't volunteer anything," Nancy told Nila, remembering what Cecilia had said about the way Nila treated the servants. "I asked him to tell me about the family. You see, Mr. Pierce—"

"I know all about it," she told Nancy. "Charles told me he'd asked you to find out what his children are up to." Her face softened a bit, and she offered her hand for Nancy to shake.

"I'm sorry to give such a rotten first impression," she said. "But you must understand, the entire staff has been against me since the day I got here. They feel threatened by the fact that a newcomer like me is now in charge of the household. At any rate, if you want to know the truth about things, you'd better talk to *me.*"

"That's why I came by," Nancy assured her. Nila smiled suddenly, and Nancy caught a glimpse of warmth she hadn't suspected was there. "So tell me how all this happened. I understand you think somebody tried to kill you?"

"You saw it yourself," Nila said insistently. "If they hadn't pumped my stomach last night, I might have died."

Nancy didn't mention the fact that Nila's stomach was sufficiently recovered to handle a healthy breakfast. "Why don't we start at the beginning?" Nancy suggested. "How did you meet Mr. Pierce?"

"I came to the States from Iceland practically penniless," Nila told her, "and went into the health care profession. I eventually got a job taking care of Charles after he had his first heart attack. We got to know each other quite well, and he soon confided in me, telling me how heartbroken he was over the way his children had rejected him.

"We fell in love, as you already know, and when Charles came home, I came with him. That's when things started to go wrong."

"How do you mean?" Nancy asked.

Nila sighed deeply. "His children suddenly showed up, out of nowhere. Karen with her new husband, and Philip, too. When Charles rebuffed their new professions of affection and continued to grow closer to me, they began to see me as the enemy.

"I learned that Philip had gone through his inheritance from his mother, and that Karen had given all her money to Jack, who'd squandered it on some stupid restaurant. Charles insisted on helping them all, even allowing Eleanor and that daughter of hers to stay on indefinitely. But they're all greedy, you see. They want it all. And they won't stop at anything to get it."

"You're referring to the letter Mr. Pierce showed me?" Nancy asked.

"Yes," Nila replied. "When Charles and I first fell in love, he changed his will to include me. I believe I was to get a fifth of the estate, the same as his other heirs and foundation.

"The family hated the fact that I was horning in on their inheritance, and they treated me terribly. Charles grew angry with them over it, and over the way they were wasting what money they already had. So he changed his will again. This time he gave me a full third. The foundation got another third, and the last third was to be split between the other heirs."

"Quite a comedown," Nancy remarked. "Did the family know about the change?"

"Oh, yes," Nila told her. "Charles wanted them to know. He hoped it would make them change their ways, but it seemed to have the opposite effect. Because that's when I got the letter. It enraged Charles, and he told me he was going to cut them out altogether. I begged him not to do that. After all, they're his family, no matter how badly they've behaved. Although I do think, to tell you the truth, that being on their own would be the best thing for all of them. They'd learn to be self-reliant, to find out what it's like to work for a living.

"Still, I felt badly about the way things were going and tried to talk Charles out of the new changes. But he wouldn't budge. At last I persuaded him to hire someone to investigate before he signed the new will. And, well, here you are."

Nancy had to wonder just how hard Nila had tried to dissuade Charles Pierce from changing his will. "I know you think Mr. Pierce's children have wasted the money they inherited," Nancy said. "And I understand you feel they've treated you badly. But what about Eleanor and Cecilia?"

"Them? Oh, they're harmless, I suppose. Overprotected, if you ask me—Eleanor should go back to school and learn some skills, but she's too spoiled to try. And her poor daughter's going to turn out the same way."

"I see," Nancy said, waiting to see if there was more.

There was. "The only thing that irritates me about Eleanor is her habit of listening behind closed doors," Nila said. "She's always digging about to find secrets. Probably knows a lot of interesting things, if you can ever worm them out of her." Again, Nila flashed Nancy a warm smile. "Really. You ought to try talking with her."

"I'll do that," Nancy promised her. "And please tell Mr. Pierce to call me as soon as he's feeling better. I'd like to speak with him."

"Of course," Nila said, getting up and shaking Nancy's hand again. "It was a pleasure meeting you, Ms. Drew. I hope your investigation will be successful."

"Thank you," Nancy said. "And, please, don't hold it against the butler that he chatted with me. I'd feel awful if you did—"

"Oh, don't worry," Nila assured her, smiling. "I won't. Really, I'm all bark and no bite."

As Nancy headed home, she puzzled over what she'd learned. While Nila Kirkedottir did not act as if she had anything to hide, she seemed to Nancy to be a woman of many faces. Nancy wondered which face was the real one.

Philip Pierce called her just after noon to confirm their date.

"Philip," Nancy said, remembering how much Bess wanted to get involved in the Pierce case, "how would you feel about double-dating tonight?"

"Double-dating?" he repeated, sounding reluctant and disappointed. "Why? Don't trust yourself alone with me?"

"It's not that," Nancy assured him, chuckling softly. "It's just—well, you and I barely know each other, and I do have a boyfriend, even though he is out of town most of the time."

"I see . . ."

"Besides, you'll love my friend Bess. She's lots of fun, and you can tell whoever you bring that he won't be sorry. She's blond and blue eyed and really cute and—"

"Okay, okay." Philip laughed. "I get the picture, Nancy. I guess I can find someone, if you insist. But next time it's just the two of us, okay?"

"Okay," she agreed. "I promise."

"Good," he said. "And I think I know who I'm going to bring tonight. I owe him a favor. From what you say, a date with your friend Bess ought to qualify."

After hanging up, Nancy called Bess and told her they were on for seven o'clock.

Bess arrived at six-thirty and paced the room excitedly while Nancy got dressed. Nancy chose a slinky red minidress and matching pumps, and was just putting the finishing touches on her makeup when Philip pulled up behind the wheel of a Maserati convertible promptly at seven. He wore an open-necked silk shirt under a dark blue blazer, and he was more gorgeous than Nancy remembered.

"Wow!" Nancy said, once again feeling herself tingling all over as she sat in the passenger seat beside him. "This car must have set you back a bit, huh?"

"A bit," he acknowledged. "But, hey— money's for spending, right? Hello, there," he greeted Bess. "Are all your friends this gorgeous, Nancy?"

Bess caught Nancy's eye and bit her lip, looking skyward, to indicate that Philip was a total hunk.

Philip drove them to an elegant restaurant on the west side of River Heights. "This used to be

Jack's place," he told Nancy. "But he ran it into the ground in three short months, if you can believe it. Anyway, it looks much better now than when he had it."

"Why do I get the impression you don't like your brother-in-law?" Nancy asked as he opened the car door to let her and Bess out.

"Because I don't," Philip said with a disarming smile. "Why should I like him? He's vain, selfish, greedy, and lazy, and he went through my sister's inheritance so fast she didn't know what hit her. She still thinks he's the greatest thing since sliced bread. Karen always was kind of naive."

"I see. Well, I guess that answers that." Actually, Nancy was full of questions she wanted to ask Philip, but she knew she'd better wait till later in the evening, when she could get him alone.

They went inside, and Philip gave his name to the maitre d', who led them to their table. "Ah, there's Tom!" Philip said, pointing to a young guy sitting at a table in the corner. Seeing them, the young man got up and waved.

Nancy froze in her tracks, stifling a gasp. Could it be? Yes, she was almost certain—Tom was the intruder she'd caught the night before breaking into Charles Pierce's desk!

Chapter

Six

"Nancy, Bess—I'd like you to meet my friend Tom Walczek," Philip said, introducing the long-haired guy.

Tom's gaze toward Nancy was piercing and intent. She wondered if he recognized her. It had been pretty dark in Pierce's study, but he would have been in there awhile, and his eyes might have adjusted enough to pick out her features.

Nancy couldn't have sworn it was him—she'd seen only his profile as he ran out—but she would have bet on it. She wondered what his connection was to Philip and whether Philip had sent him to steal the draft copy of his father's new will.

They all quickly fell into conversation, with Bess and Philip doing most of the talking. Bess was in a great mood, Nancy could tell, and she obviously thought that both Philip and Tom were real hunks.

Tom was friendly enough, but every once in a while Nancy would catch him glancing at her, and she detected an aura of discomfort and nervousness about him.

He had rougher edges than Philip, and Nancy sensed that he'd led a hard life. If he was well off now, Nancy guessed, he must have made his money on his own, not had it handed to him.

"So, Tom," Bess asked, as the waiter went off with their orders. "What do you do?"

"Me?" Tom replied. "I'm in the entertainment business."

"Oh," Bess said enthusiastically. "Are you an actor? You look familiar. Have I seen you on TV or something? You know, you look a lot like that guy on *Tomorrow Is Another Day.*"

"Uh, no, I'm not an actor. I own a club," Tom explained. Nancy thought he was reluctant to answer.

"That's great!" Bess exclaimed. "Can we go there later?"

Tom shifted uncomfortably, and Philip quickly came to his rescue. "Bess, Tom and I have already made plans for the rest of our evening together. But maybe some other time?"

"Sure, some other time," Tom echoed.

"Tonight we're going dancing," Philip explained. "At the Ace of Clubs. Right, Tom?"

"Right," Tom said, smiling, as the waiter arrived with their appetizers.

Nancy knew the Ace of Clubs. It was a great

place to go dancing. She and Ned had been there once or twice, and she felt a twinge of guilt about going there without Ned. But she told herself it was part of an investigation, and that made it okay—sort of.

As for this restaurant, she'd certainly never been in it before. It was out of her price range. Philip was obviously a regular because he knew the menu well and insisted they order several appetizers, despite the cost. Nancy figured she and Bess could buy several new outfits for the price of their dinners.

The rest of the meal went well, and soon the foursome found themselves dancing at the Ace of Clubs. Definitely the hottest spot in River Heights, Nancy decided. At one point Nancy and Bess started off to the ladies' room to freshen up.

"Hurry back, Drew!" Philip called after her.

Maybe it was the mention of her last name— but when she turned to wave at Philip, Nancy saw that Tom was whispering something in Philip's ear. Philip's expression darkened, but when he noticed her staring at him, his smile returned.

A couple of numbers later, Nancy said, "I'm going to step outside for a breath of fresh air. It's kind of hot in here—and my ears need a rest, too."

"I'll come with you," Philip offered. As soon as they were outside, his expression became grim. "So," he said, "you're a detective. Why didn't you tell me?"

That was what Tom had told him. Nancy bit her lip but didn't answer immediately.

"Is that why you agreed to go out with me?" he pressed her.

"That wasn't the only reason," she said, gazing into his eyes. "Please, you mustn't think it was. I—I wanted to go out with you." As she said the words, Nancy realized they were true.

He returned her gaze with one of his own, as if he were looking deep inside her for the answer to his question. Then, slowly, he took her in his arms and kissed her, his lips just brushing hers at first. Soon, though, the kiss grew more passionate. It lingered on and on, and when it was over, and he drew back, Nancy had to catch her breath. He had taken her by surprise, but she had to admit to herself that she'd wanted him to kiss her—that she had enjoyed it, even more than she'd thought she would.

"Philip . . . I—"

"You don't have to say anything if you don't want to," he assured her. "I understand. The old man hired you to check up on me, and that's what you were doing. Anyway, I believe you now. You really did want to come out with me. Kisses don't lie."

Nancy smiled shyly and nodded her agreement. "Who told you I was a detective? Tom?" She remembered seeing her name scribbled in Pierce's notebook—*N. Drew, investigator* . . . Had Philip's mention of her last name clued Tom in?

Philip seemed puzzled. "I saw Tom whispering

to you as we went to the bathroom," Nancy admitted, explaining how she'd figured it out. "I guessed he was telling you about me, judging by your reaction."

"Oh. Right," Philip said sheepishly.

"Any idea *how* he knew who I was?" Nancy asked innocently.

"He, er, he didn't have time to explain how he heard about you," Philip said. "I just figured Jack told him. They're friends. In fact, that's how I met Tom. The two of them go way back."

"I see," Nancy said. "So, now that you know I'm a detective, what's your reaction?"

Philip grinned slyly. "I'm not going to let it ruin our time together. The old man wants you to check me out? So what? It's easy to figure out why. He wants you to see if I deserve to be included in his new will. Right?"

"Something like that," Nancy admitted. "Do you?"

"Of course I do," he said with his signature grin. "I deserve every penny. Besides, I need it. I'll be perfectly honest with you, since you're bound to find out sooner or later anyway. I've gone through every penny my mother left me. I'm flat broke. Awful, isn't it?"

"But the car?" Nancy said. "And tonight— how will you—"

"Tom's been lending me money," Philip explained. "Remember I told you I owed him a favor? Jack introduced us a couple of years ago, when I needed a loan pretty badly."

"I thought you didn't like Jack," Nancy said. "Why would Jack help you out?"

"We liked each other better back then," Philip explained. "That was before he squandered all of Karen's money. At any rate, Tom was perfectly willing to lend me some. He's made me several loans since, and he knows I'm good for it eventually. When I inherit my share, I'll pay back every penny. Unlike my mother's fortune, my father's is virtually unlimited."

"I see," Nancy said. It was the first unattractive thing Philip had said in her presence, and it took her aback. He really did need an attitude adjustment, she thought to herself.

"Oh, I know what you're thinking," Philip said with a sigh. "I'm nothing but an opportunist, a leech, a good-for-nothing—"

"Well . . ."

"It's all true," he said with puppy dog eyes that were impossible to resist. "I just can't seem to help spending money when I've got it, that's my problem. I ran through the money my mother left me in just two years or so. I dropped out of college and spent my way into poverty. I don't know what I would have done next. But as it happened, Dad got sick right about then. So I moved back into my childhood home to be close to him."

Nancy scowled. "It sounds so callous," she said. "As if you wanted to be close to his money, not him. You've got to admit, it sounds that way."

"There's more to it, though," Philip protested.

"To be brutally honest, I've never really forgiven my father for the way he treated my mother. Neither has Karen. He was so cold to Mom, so hard. She settled for much less money than she should have. And even when she got so sick, he never came to visit her—not once."

Philip swallowed hard, and Nancy could see that the memory upset him. "He sent us cards on our birthdays every year, without fail," he went on. "Always with a check—but no signature on the card. I think he had the servants send them. And never once did he invite us to visit him."

Philip had been gazing down at the ground, but now he looked straight at Nancy. "No, I don't much like the old man, to answer your next question. Why should I? He was always so absorbed in building that company of his— always so distant with me and Karen—so hard on Mother. Still, I did feel bad when he got sick . . ."

"So you moved back into the mansion," Nancy finished for him. "Your father gave you an allowance, but you spent it so fast that he threatened to cut you off."

"Right," Philip said, his voice bitter.

"It must have come as quite a shock to you," Nancy said, "to see how close your father was with Nila."

Philip's eyes grew hard. "I hated her from the first," he confided. "She's an ice-cold woman. She makes the old man look like a loveable fuzzy bear by comparison. And she hates all of us. I suppose she feels threatened. You see, I'm convinced that she plans to inherit all Dad's money herself."

"So you don't think her feelings for him are genuine?" Nancy asked.

"Get real!" Philip exploded. "Do you? A gorgeous young woman like her, and a sick old man like him? She's with him for his money plain and simple! And he's totally blinded by her, which is why he hired you. She's convinced him we're no good. And now she's got him thinking one of us is trying to kill her!"

"Is she right?" Nancy asked pointedly. "I mean, if she does have designs on your father's fortune, you'd all have a strong motive for getting rid of her. . . ."

"You're the detective. I'll leave it to you to make up your own mind. But I can tell you right now—Nila's faking the whole thing. The letter, that fainting spell the other night—they're all baloney."

"I'll certainly be looking into it," Nancy assured him.

Philip's expression softened, and he smiled sheepishly at her. "Sorry I went off like that," he said. "But it was kind of a shock to find out you were a detective. Listen, I'll be happy to help you investigate, in any way I can. I certainly didn't try to kill her. And if Jack did, he should get what's coming to him."

"All right," Nancy said. "Tell me about Jack. Why don't you like him? There's more, isn't there? More than you've already told me."

"It's the way he treats Karen," Philip said

grudgingly. "Disappearing all the time, sometimes even all night. Lately Karen's been totally out of her mind over it." He shook his head. "Let's just say there are things I wish I didn't know about him."

Nancy waited for more, but Philip seemed to think he'd already said too much. She nodded thoughtfully. "Okay," she said. "I'll check it out. And now," she added, slipping her arm through his, "I think you'd better take me home."

Philip drove Nancy home in the Maserati, while Tom and Bess stayed behind to dance more.

From her front door, Nancy watched Philip drive away. She felt a warm wave wash over her at the memory of his kisses, both the first one and the one they'd just shared. It had been softer, more tender than the first.

Nancy knew she had to put a check on her emotions. She liked this guy a lot, probably too much for her own good, and she had an investigation to conduct. An investigation in which Philip Pierce was a prime suspect.

Nancy went to bed, but it was hours before she was able to fall asleep. When she woke up the next morning, she was tempted to call Bess, to see how the rest of her night had gone. Nancy didn't trust Tom—breaking into someone's desk was serious business—and she worried about Bess spending time with a guy like that.

In the end Nancy decided it was too early to call Bess. Instead, she decided to ride over to

Karen and Jack's house and have a talk with one or both of them. Philip Pierce had been very forthcoming. She wondered if his sister and brother-in-law would be, too.

After a quick breakfast, Nancy hopped into her Mustang convertible and took off for the other side of town. The case occupied her thoughts, but she did notice that the car was behaving a little abnormally—wobbling, sort of. Weird. She decided to take it in to be checked later that day.

She rounded the corner of Main and River Streets, turning left. That was when she felt the wheel go.

All at once, as she swung to the left, the front right tire, wheel and all, went bounding away from the car. The Mustang's axle hit the road with a jolt. Before Nancy knew what was happening, her car was skidding totally out of control—and heading right for a telephone pole!

Chapter

Seven

NANCY KNEW that hitting the brakes would do her no good at all. She turned the wheel hard to the right, taking the car in the direction it was already going, knowing that the only way to right her skid with three wheels was to use the Mustang's natural momentum.

Car brakes screeched all around her, horns sounded, and pedestrians ran for safety as Nancy's car careened across the intersection. Her maneuvering caused the car to swerve to the right of the telephone pole and jump up onto a broad, empty sidewalk. It hit a garbage can with a loud bang, spun around twice, and came to rest just inches short of three terrified passersby.

As soon as her heart was beating normally again, Nancy hopped out of the vehicle and rushed to see that the three pedestrians were all right. They seemed to be merely shaken up. They were a little angry until they saw that one of the car's wheels had come completely off. The lone wheel now lay on the other side of the wide avenue.

Traffic had come to a complete halt, and a police siren sounded nearby. People were talking excitedly about the accident, and Nancy was just glad to be alive. She knew very well how close she had come to dying—or to killing somebody else.

A squad car pulled up, and a young police officer she happened to know got out and came over to her. "What happened, miss—why, Nancy—it's you!"

"Hi, Officer Kelly," Nancy said. "One of my wheels came right off the axle. Lucky thing nobody was hurt."

"I'll say," said the officer, scribbling in a notepad. Whipping out his walkie-talkie, he called headquarters, then put in a call for a tow truck.

Nancy bent down to look at her axle. It seemed to have survived the skid pretty much intact. She couldn't see anything wrong with it at first glance.

"You ought to keep that car in better shape, Nancy," Officer Kelly scolded her.

"But I do," Nancy protested. "I mean, I did. Just last month I had it tuned up and inspected."

"Hmmm," the officer said, bending down to examine the axle himself.

Glancing down the street, Nancy saw the tow truck coming. She crossed the avenue and rolled the wheel back across to her car.

"This is so weird," she said as a gangly young guy with long, greasy hair got out of the tow truck and came over to them. The sign on his truck read Bud's Auto Body and Towing.

"Hey, what's up, Kelly?" he asked.

"Check this out, Skeeter," Officer Kelly said, pointing his flashlight at the axle. "Seems okay to me, but the wheel came right off it."

Skeeter bent down to look, then straightened up and scratched his head. "Hmmm—wait a sec," he said, then went over to his truck bed, returning with a screwdriver. Bending over, he pried the hubcap off the loose wheel. "Look here," he said. "Here's the problem. Four out of the five lug nuts are missing, and the fifth must have been loose. No wonder the wheel came off!"

Nancy blinked in astonishment, her mind racing.

"Whoa!" Officer Kelly exclaimed. "It's amazing you got this far," he said. "You sure you've been riding around okay? I mean, no flat tires or anything?"

"Nothing," Nancy said, shaking her head.

"Well, lug nuts don't just disappear," Skeeter said definitively. "Somebody took that wheel off, and when they put it back on, they just stuck the hubcap on without putting four of the nuts back." He shook his head disapprovingly. "I'll tell you, some guys just don't care what kind of work they do."

"All right, hook it up and take it in," Kelly

said, and Skeeter pulled up the tow truck. "When was the last time anyone took off that wheel, Nancy?"

"I can't even remember," Nancy said. "Months and months ago, certainly."

"And you've been driving around like this since then?"

"I don't think so," Nancy told him. "I think something must have happened to it very recently."

Skeeter had hooked up her Mustang to the tow truck, and Nancy climbed into the cab with him. Kelly stuffed his pad into his pocket. "Be careful from now on, okay? It's important to take care of your car."

"I know, Officer Kelly," Nancy assured him. "Boy, do I know."

From the body shop, Nan called Bess to ask her to lend her her car. Bess was less than happy about lending Nancy her car for the day, though.

"I just got it washed and detailed, Nan," Bess complained when she picked her up. "What if whoever sabotaged your car tries again on mine?"

"Bess," Nancy assured her, "didn't anyone ever tell you lightning never strikes twice in the same place? Trust me—I'll take good care of your baby for you."

"Oh, all right," Bess grumbled, getting into the passenger seat so that Nancy could drop her off at home.

"How was the rest of your evening with Tom, by the way?" Nancy asked as they drove.

"Pretty good," Bess said. "He seems like a fun guy. The only thing was, he seemed to be more curious about you than he was about me."

"Hmm," Nancy said, scowling. "I'm not surprised."

"Why? Oh, Nan—you don't think he's the one who tinkered with your car, do you? That would be so horrible!"

"Well, I don't know, Bess. It's a possibility, but there are lots of others. That's what I'm going to try to find out today. But one thing's for sure," she concluded as they pulled up in front of Bess's house. "Someone's upset that I'm investigating the Pierce family—upset enough to try to kill me."

After dropping Bess off, Nancy headed back to the address Philip had given her for Karen and Jack's house. She wanted to interview them about the Pierce family situation, since she hadn't really had a chance to talk with them at the party.

The house was a modest split-level on a quiet side street in one of River Heights's better neighborhoods. Just as Nancy pulled up, she saw Jack emerge from the house, holding a large briefcase in his right hand. He was furtively glancing around, as if he were sneaking out and wanted to make sure he wasn't being observed. Nancy decided to follow him.

61

Jack got into a beautifully maintained Thunderbird convertible from the sixties and took off down the street with a roar. It was all Nancy could do to keep up in Bess's little compact, but she didn't want to take any unnecessary chances driving her friend's car.

She followed Jack at a safe distance because she realized from the way he'd left his house that he'd notice anyone tailing him. He drove across town, passing the railroad station, and entered an industrial section of River Heights. Nancy was getting more and more curious. She was sure that Jack was up to something.

He slowed down outside a large, low building set among warehouses and railroad tracks.

Nancy pulled over about a hundred yards behind him, and whipped out her mini-binoculars to observe his movements.

Jack carried the briefcase to the door of the building and rang the buzzer. Moments later the door opened to admit Jack, then shut behind him.

Nancy knew there was no time to lose. She got out of the car and ran toward the building. The windows along the front were boarded up, but there was a little chink in one of the boards. She crept close to it and peered through, hoping to get a glimpse of what was going on inside.

She was lucky and could just make out Jack giving the briefcase to a man she didn't recognize, but one she wouldn't have wanted to meet in a dark alley. He had a brutish, scarred face and massive hands. When the man opened the briefcase, Nancy gasped. It was full of cash!

The man nodded and shook Jack's hand. Nancy guessed that this transaction concluded Jack's business and that he would be leaving. She ducked around the corner of the building to avoid being seen. Sure enough, a few seconds later Jack emerged, got into his car, and drove off.

Nancy came out of her hiding place, determined to find out what sort of place this was. She stepped up to the front door and pressed the buzzer.

An eye studied her through the peephole. Then the door opened a crack, and the brutish face looked out at her suspiciously. "Yeah? What do you want?"

Thinking fast, Nancy whipped out her wallet and waved it at him. If money had talked in Jack's case, maybe it would work for her, too.

The man scratched his head. "How'd you hear of this place?"

"Jack Oliver told me about you," she fibbed.

"Hmmm. Okay—which team you want to bet on?" he asked.

So, it was an illegal sports betting parlor! And clearly, Jack was up to his neck in it.

"I'm not sure," Nancy said. "I'd like to have a look at the sheet for today. Can I come inside?"

The man was uncertain. "I dunno," he said. "Since you're a new customer, I'd better clear it with the boss. Wait here a second."

He slammed the door in her face and left
Nancy waiting there for a full three minutes.
When the door opened again, the man with the
brutish face had someone else with him—
someone Nancy had seen before.

It was Tom Walczek!

Chapter

Eight

WELL, IF IT ISN'T NANCY DREW!" Tom said, his expression quickly changing from one of surprise. "This lady's a detective, Vinnie. And a pretty good one, it seems. She tracked us down." He shot a glance at his companion, who ominously reached a hand inside his coat pocket.

Nancy thought about confronting him with breaking into Charles Pierce's desk the other night, but seeing the glint of metal in Vinnie's hand, she decided against it.

"I, uh, I was looking for Jack. I thought he might be here."

"He isn't," Tom said. "And let me say that I hope, as a *private* detective, you'll keep this little encounter to yourself—understand?"

"Perfectly," Nancy said, slowly backing away. "I'm investigating something else entirely.

65

Whatever you're up to here is no business of mine," she assured him.

"I'm glad to hear that. And by the way," Tom called out to her before shutting the door, "give my regards to your friend Bess. She's a real babe."

Nancy hightailed it out of there, heading straight for the Pierce mansion. She made it in under ten minutes. She pulled up beside Philip's Maserati and saw Philip himself giving instructions to one of the servants, who was busily waxing the car.

"Nancy," he said, waving as she stepped out of Bess's car. "I didn't expect to see you again this soon. Tell me you couldn't stay away from me for another minute."

Nancy shook her head. "Not quite, Philip," she said. "Can we talk in private?" she asked, nodding toward the servant.

"Definitely," he said, leading her around to the rear of the house and into the gazebo that was set in the middle of a rose garden. "Now," he said as they settled in next to each other on a wooden bench. "Tell me. What's up?"

"For starters," Nancy began, "someone tried to kill me this morning."

Philip's reaction was as shocked as she hoped it would be. She went on to explain about her car, and his face showed all the proper concern. But Nancy wondered just how good an actor Philip Pierce was.

"Are you sure?" he asked her. "Couldn't those lug nuts have come off by themselves?"

"Not a chance," Nancy assured him. "Someone who knows I'm a detective doesn't want me investigating your family."

"Mmmm," Philip said, nodding. "I can see where you'd think it would be me. But, Nancy, I'd never do anything to hurt you. I like you—a lot!"

There was that smile of his again. Nancy felt herself softening, hooked by the spell of his warm glance. She found it impossible to believe he was lying to her. But experience told her that charming people were often the very best liars.

"Besides, I was with you yesterday evening, and after I dropped you off, I came straight back here and went to bed, like a good little boy."

"I don't suppose anyone can verify that," Nancy said.

"Of course not," Philip said, shrugging. "And even if they could, I suppose I could have driven back to your house at any time during the night and sabotaged your car. But then, any of us could have."

"True," Nancy agreed. "Philip, tell me about your friend Tom."

"Friend? He's not my friend. Our relationship is strictly business. But why do you ask? Is Bess already crazy about him?"

Nancy told him everything that had happened that morning. Philip didn't seem surprised.

"You know," he said, sighing, "I did think twice before calling Tom. But you did ask to double at the last minute, and he was the only

67

guy I could think of. I guess you could say he doesn't exactly have a sterling character. . . ."

"You could say that," Nancy agreed.

"Sorry," Philip said. "Hey, it was only one date, right? Besides, he's good-looking and single."

"I don't think he's Bess's type," Nancy said sternly. "She doesn't go in for criminals."

"Mmmm," Philip said, biting his lip.

"So how are you mixed up with him?" Nancy asked.

"Me? I told you, he's a friend of Jack's. That's how I met him."

"From the looks of things," Nancy said, "I wouldn't call him Jack's friend—more like his bookie."

"I guess you're right," Philip acknowledged. "You know, I'm convinced that's how Jack ran through all the money Karen inherited."

"I thought you said they invested it in a restaurant," Nancy said.

"True—but remember the place went under in just a few months, in spite of the fact that it was packed most nights. I suspect Jack was skimming the profits and using them to make bets. He's always had big dreams. Unfortunately, he's not lucky, and I think he blew most of Karen's fortune at that 'club' of Tom's."

He sighed bitterly. "If I had more guts, I'd tell Karen all about it, too," he said. "But I know it would break her heart, and I could never do that to her—I care for her too much. Besides, if I ratted on Jack, he might get Tom to call in my loans. And then where would I be?"

"I see," Nancy said, getting up. "One more question, Philip. Did you hire Tom to steal your father's new will?"

Philip appeared flabbergasted. "Huh?" he asked. "What are you talking about?"

"I caught him breaking into your dad's desk during the engagement party," Nancy explained.

"Well, ask Jack about it, not me," Philip said heatedly, more upset than Nancy had ever seen him. "Look, I may not be a perfect son, and I'm certainly no angel. But I wouldn't ask somebody to steal my old man's will, or try to kill my future stepmother. And I certainly wouldn't try to kill a detective I'm crazy about."

It was impossible to doubt the sincerity in his eyes. Nancy decided she was too emotionally involved with Philip to judge the truth of his words and that she'd better focus elsewhere for the moment.

"Hey!" he called after her as she left the gazebo. "Where are you going?"

"To snoop around," she replied with a little smile. "It's my job, remember? See you later, Philip." Nancy gave him a wink as she left.

Going around to the side of the house, she noticed that a side door had been left slightly ajar. Nancy quietly let herself in and found herself in a storage area piled high with provisions of all kinds. Mr. Pierce was clearly a man who liked to entertain large numbers of guests.

Nancy was about to step into the hall when she heard hushed voices coming from there. One she recognized as Karen's. The other, the more hesitant one, was Eleanor's. Nancy put her ear to the door to hear better.

"But can't you see we've got to do something before it's too late?" Karen was pleading. "Look, Ellie, Phil's already agreed. We're going to Dad and demand that he look into Nila's past before he marries her."

"I'm just not sure," Eleanor hedged. "With Charles's health, it might be just the thing that pushes him over the edge. His heart is so weak. Besides, if we make him angry, he might cut us out of his will. Not that I care, for myself—but Cecilia . . ."

"But, Ellie, what about that newspaper article?" Karen protested. "Besides, if Dad goes ahead and marries Nila, how long do you think it'll be before she makes him get rid of us? Where will you go? What will you do?"

"Oh, Charles would never do that," Eleanor protested. "Not as long as we're good to him."

"Wouldn't he?" Karen challenged her. "Look at the way she's got him wrapped around her little finger. She already rules this house. How long do you think it's going to be, once she's got that ring on her finger and her name in his will, before she kicks you out?"

"Oh—oh, I just don't know. . . ."

"Mother." That was Cecilia's voice. So all three of them were together, Nancy noted. "I think you should listen to Karen. She knows him better than you do. She's Uncle Charles's daughter, after all."

Eleanor's voice grew suddenly more decisive. "You're right, Karen," she said. "Something does have to be done. I'll go ahead and speak to him, then. You do want me to be the one who tells him, don't you?"

"Naturally," Karen replied. "He doesn't trust Philip or me."

"When?" Eleanor asked.

"After lunch," Karen pressed her. "And don't put it off any longer. There's that detective you told us about, remember?"

So Eleanor *had* told Karen and Jack about her. Nancy realized what this meant—everyone in the Pierce family knew what she was up to, and therefore had a reason to want to get rid of her. Nancy had suspected all along that Eleanor was a collector of secrets, but she'd thought the timid woman would be better at holding on to them.

The voices had ceased. Figuring that the trio must have wandered away, Nancy inched open the door to find an empty hallway. Not wanting to wait for the others to talk to Pierce before she gave him her report, she went in search of him.

Pierce was not in his study. The desk was still in a state of disarray. Clearly, he hadn't been in there since the night of the party. Nancy wondered if his health had kept him from conducting any business since then. If so, he would probably be in his bedroom.

Nancy spotted one of the older servant women emerging from the parlor and asked directions to

Mr. Pierce's suite. She pointed her up the main staircase and to the left. Nancy proceeded down a luxuriously carpeted hallway with floor-to-ceiling windows that looked out on the gardens behind the house.

Pierce's suite was at the far end of the hallway. As she approached, the door opened. Nancy ducked behind a heavy, brocaded curtain. Nila Kirkedottir emerged, pushing a cart full of medicines and medical instruments. She pushed the cart past Nancy, never noticing her.

Nancy tiptoed forward as soon as Nila was out of sight. She knocked on the door of Pierce's suite, and when he called out for her to come in, she entered. She found him sitting up in bed, reading a newspaper.

"Ah, Nancy!" he exclaimed, laying down the paper as he saw her. His greeting was hearty, and he actually seemed in decent health. He was certainly much better than he'd been the night Nila had lain unconscious on the floor. "Have you come to report to me on your investigation?"

"Yes, sir," Nancy replied. After seating herself in a chair, she proceeded to tell him what she'd found out about his heirs.

Pierce's face reddened with anger as she spoke. When she had finished, he flung his rolled-up newspaper down onto the floor and raised his fists in the air. "I knew it!" he cried in fury. "They're just no good. Gambling away their money, spending it like water, stealing the new draft of my will, poisoning my Nila . . . I'll cut them all off without a penny!"

"Mr. Pierce—" Nancy said, trying to interrupt. But Pierce was already punching in a number on his phone.

"Get me Bishop," he said. "Tell him I want him here this afternoon. I'm going ahead with the changes in my will, and this time I mean it." He slammed down the phone on the bedside table.

"Mr. Pierce," Nancy cautioned him, "I think you should hear the rest of my report."

"Why bother?" he asked. "You've told me all I need to know. My heirs are a bunch of no-good spongers!"

"Maybe so," Nancy said. "But that doesn't mean they're trying to kill Nila. In fact, my friend at the police lab tells me there was nothing but cranberry juice in her glass that night."

"What?" Pierce stared at her, frozen.

"That's right," Nancy told him. "Which might lead one to think that, much as I hate to suggest this, Nila might be faking things. Like that letter. She could conceivably have written it herself."

"Listen, young lady," Pierce said, wagging a finger at her. "I won't have you insulting the woman I'm going to marry. Tell me, have you even bothered to talk with Nila?"

"Yes, I have," Nancy assured him. "She's a very intelligent, capable woman, obviously. But I've seen her temper, too, and I think it's pretty clear that Nila feels persecuted around here."

"Justifiably so," Pierce protested.

"True," Nancy agreed. "The family isn't exactly wild about her, and neither are some of the staff. But I think Nila may be exaggerating things in her own mind. Maybe to the point where she finds herself justified in making the others look bad in your eyes. Look, Mr. Pierce, all I'm saying is, give me another day or two to look into things before you act on this."

"Young lady," Pierce said, his face slowly returning to its normal color, "you go ahead and keep looking into things. But in the meantime, I'm drawing up a new will. And if you haven't found out anything new in twenty-four hours, I'm going to sign it." He lay back in bed and waved her off, signifying that their interview was over.

Nancy backed away and opened the door, retreating into the anteroom of the suite. As she did, she saw a closet door close. Someone had been eavesdropping!

Nancy silently walked over to the door and, placing her hand on the knob, suddenly yanked it open. There, gasping in horror, her hand to her mouth, was Eleanor!

Chapter

Nine

"Hello there," Nancy said casually. She offered Eleanor a helping hand, and the woman emerged from the closet. "Doing a little spring cleaning?"

"I'm—I'm afraid you've caught me snooping," Eleanor confessed, her face flushing. "I'm sorry. You see, I happened to be on my way to speak to my brother about a very urgent matter, and, well, I heard you two talking in there, and Charles was being so loud, I couldn't help overhearing. . . ."

"And what he was saying had a lot to do with why you wanted to speak with him, am I right?" Nancy guessed, guiding Eleanor out into the hallway.

"Why, yes!" Eleanor gasped. "How did you know?"

75

"I've been doing a little snooping around myself," Nancy admitted. "Something about Nila's past, wasn't it?"

"Yes," Eleanor said, nodding conspiratorially. "You see, a couple of days ago someone showed me a newspaper article from the Stockton *Gazette*. It was all about how Nila had stolen money from her previous employer."

"Who was it who showed you the article?" Nancy asked pointedly.

Eleanor seemed to shrink back into herself. "Oh—I'm not sure I should say. No, I don't think that would be right. I wouldn't want to get anyone else into trouble. Charles is angry enough as it is."

"You've got that right," Nancy agreed.

"But you see, I wanted very much to tell Charles about it," Eleanor explained. "Because it might affect his future, too, you see."

"And yours as well," Nancy pointed out.

"Yes, I suppose so. At any rate, Nila must have faked her letter of recommendation from her previous employer's children, because they would never have written one for a person who had stolen from them. So, of course, Nila came here under false pretenses! And I felt it was my duty to inform Charles about her."

"Why not just show him the article?" Nancy asked.

"Well, I don't have it," Eleanor admitted. "And I'm not sure where it is just now. But it will be easy enough for Charles to check into it himself. Or to ask Nila about, although I'm sure she'll deny everything. But you see, the article had her picture in it and everything. So denying it won't do her any good."

"Hmmm . . . I'd like to see that article myself," Nancy said. "Do you think you could find it and show it to me later today?"

"I could try," Eleanor said with a weak smile. "As for Charles," she added, her face pale, "perhaps now is not the best time to talk with him about it. He seems so agitated. I don't want to risk his health in any way. Perhaps later, if I can find the article, *you* could show it to him?"

"We'll see," Nancy said. "Why don't you go find it first? Then we'll discuss who shows it to him."

Eleanor went off quickly, obviously grateful to escape. Nancy went back downstairs, with the new development weighing heavily on her mind. In spite of all their faults, could Pierce's family be right about Nila?

Nancy left the house and headed out to Bess's car. As she was getting behind the wheel, she heard someone call her name. Nancy rolled down the window and saw Karen trotting over to her, a tennis racket in her hand.

"Hi!" she greeted Nancy cheerfully. "How are things going?"

Nancy gave her a long look. "How do you mean that, exactly?" she asked.

"Oh. I forgot," Karen said. "You don't know that I know—I mean, about your being a detective. Eleanor couldn't stop blabbing about it to everyone after you left the party the other night."

"I see," Nancy said. "Hang on a sec, will you?"

Karen stepped back so Nancy could open the car door and get out. "Got a minute?" Nancy asked.

"Sure," Karen said. "I was just playing tennis with Jack. He took the day off from work. He's got the kind of job where he can make his own hours."

"I see," Nancy said, arching an eyebrow.

Catching the subtle change in Nancy's expression, Karen became suspicious. "What is it?" she asked. "What were you thinking just then?"

"Me?" Nancy responded. "Oh, nothing."

"Please," Karen said, frowning. "I hate it when people aren't honest with me."

"Aren't people normally honest with you?" Nancy asked cautiously.

Karen sighed uncomfortably. "You know something about Jack, don't you?" she asked.

"What makes you say that?" Nancy wondered.

"When I said he makes his own hours . . . Look, just tell me, okay? If you know something about Jack that I should know, let me have it, right now."

Nancy bit her lip. "Well, if you must know, I did find something out. I spotted him at a place that turned out to be an illegal betting parlor."

Karen gasped. "When was this?" she demanded.

"This morning," Nancy replied. "He had a lot of cash on him. I'm sorry to be the one to tell you."

Karen was clearly steaming mad. "I *knew* there was something going on," she muttered under her breath. "I've been blind—totally blind!"

"Well, now, wait," Nancy cautioned. "Maybe we're jumping to conclusions here. . . ."

"No way," Karen interjected. "It all makes too much sense. All the money that disappeared those months when we had the restaurant. I'll kill him, I swear I will. To think I believed all his lame excuses. I've been a total fool!"

"Maybe this is a problem you two can work out," Nancy said in a soothing tone, trying to calm Karen.

The attempt was useless. "I'm going to wrap this tennis racket around his scheming head!" she swore. "When I think of how much I've trusted him—"

"Karen, it's not my intention to cause trouble between you two," Nancy said. "The only reason I was tracking your husband was because someone may be trying to hurt Nila—and someone definitely tried to hurt me."

Suddenly Karen turned her wrath on Nancy. "You don't know what you're talking about," she screamed, her eyes welling up with tears. "Just get out of here! Do you hear? Get out! And don't come back!"

Feeling bad that she'd upset Karen so much, Nancy got into her car. As she drove down the driveway, she saw in her rearview mirror that Jack was coming up the path toward Karen, tennis racket in hand. He put an arm on her shoulder, only to have her shake it off. The last thing Nancy saw before she turned onto the main road was Karen slamming her tennis racket onto the ground.

Without meaning to, Nancy had created a very real problem for that couple, and she had definitely made at least two of her suspects furious with her.

Maybe some good would come out of it, though—maybe something would come to the surface. Nancy sure hoped so—because even if Jack wasn't the one who'd tried to kill her before, he'd sure want to now.

"At least my car's still in one piece," Bess said cheerfully. "Not to mention you."

"Thanks." Nancy grinned. The two friends were sitting in Nancy's kitchen, sharing a late afternoon snack. "Sorry to break the bad news about Tom."

"It's okay," Bess said, making a sour face. "Actually, I'd been hoping he'd call to ask me out again. Now I won't wait around for the phone to ring."

"I kind of like Philip, too," Nancy admitted.

"Mmmm—well, he's truly awesome," Bess said, rolling her eyes. "I don't know how you can keep your mind on investigating him. Those eyes of his are totally distracting."

"Totally," Nancy agreed. "Actually, I've been feeling kind of guilty. I keep thinking about Ned—"

"Aw, Nan, give it up," Bess said. "Ned would understand—Philip's a suspect, right?"

"A *very cute* suspect, Bess."

"All right, so he's irresistible. Leaving that aside, do you really think he tried to kill Nila?"

"I'm not sure anybody tried to kill Nila," Nancy replied. "It looks as if she set the whole thing up herself to get the others in trouble with Pierce. But I can't be sure. Something about that cranberry juice still bothers me. I can't put my finger on what it is. But there's no doubt that someone tried to kill me this morning. And I'm not about to let whoever it was get away with it— even if it means nailing the cutest guy in the whole world."

Just then the phone rang. Nancy picked it up and said hello to Charles Pierce. He was inviting her to dinner that night.

"I've spoken to Bishop, and the new will's drawn up," he told her with a note of satisfaction in his voice. "He's bringing it over here this evening for me to look over before signing. The only trouble is, I need two witnesses. I can't use the family, of course. Nor the staff. I've left each of them a little something, and no one who's a beneficiary of a will can be a witness."

"Gee, Mr. Pierce," Nancy said uncomfortably. "Are you sure you— You said you'd wait twenty-four hours before signing it."

"I've changed my mind," he declared. "And don't try to talk me out of it. My family has made their own bad luck, and now they're going to have to learn to live with it. It'll be good for

81

them—teach them to make their own way in the world. After all, I did, and it didn't do me any harm. At any rate, that's why I'm inviting you—so you can witness the signing. Please don't say no. I do so appreciate the good work you've done."

Nancy was profoundly disturbed by what Pierce had just told her. She would have to take him aside to tell him about the newspaper article about Nila. Perhaps that, on top of what she'd already told him about the lab report, would shake Pierce's certainty enough for him to delay signing this new will of his. But for the moment, she decided, the best thing to do would be to accept his offer. She glanced across the table.

"Could I bring my friend Bess?" Nancy asked. "You did say you needed two witnesses, and she works with me."

"Of course, bring her along! See you both in an hour, around five," he finished, sounding extremely cheerful.

"Well, Bess," Nancy said after hanging up, "it looks like you're going to get inside the Pierce mansion sooner than you thought."

Nancy and Bess arrived at the mansion at five o'clock. The butler, noticing that Bess was staring openmouthed at the opulent furnishings, offered to escort her on a quick tour of the ground floor rooms. Bess happily accepted, and the two of them left Nancy in the hallway.

She was alone only for a moment because Jack and Karen came in from outside. Jack greeted

Nancy with an icy stare, then said, "Karen, I'm going upstairs." He trotted up the staircase, but the chill he'd cast remained behind him.

Karen sighed. "I shouldn't have blown up at you the way I did," she said to Nancy. "Jack and I have a lot to work out, I can see that now. It looks as if I've closed my eyes to a lot that was going on. I guess I owe you my thanks—it's just that it's all so shocking and painful."

"You don't have to say anything," Nancy told her. "I understand." I just hope I'm not the one who winds up paying the price, Nancy thought, recalling Jack's hateful look a moment earlier.

Just then a memory popped into Nancy's head, a memory of Jack beating up an opposing player he thought had tackled him too hard. Yes, he'd always had a temper, even back in high school.

Karen went upstairs, passing Philip on his way down. He came up to Nancy and swept her into his arms.

"Hi, gorgeous," he said, giving her a passionate kiss before Nancy could prepare herself or resist. "What's going on tonight, anyway? Did the old man tell you anything? Eleanor seems so glum, but she won't say a word about it to any of us."

"I think we're all going to find out before too long," Nancy assured him, not wanting to give away the fact that she already knew.

Eleanor and Cecilia came down the stairs, wearing serious expressions.

"Hello, Aunt Ellie," Philip said, giving her a

little kiss on the cheek. "Hi, Cecie. Look, cheer up, you two. Whatever happens, we'll all get through it."

"That's easy for you to say, Philip," Cecilia commented, taking her mother by the arm. "You've got an allowance, and you can always go find a job if you have to. But who's going to hire mother at her age and without any experience? Where are we supposed to live?" She led Eleanor into the parlor without waiting for an answer from Philip.

Philip gazed at the pair, shaking his head. "That Cecie," he said with a sigh. "It's like there's this little black cloud that follows her around wherever she goes. Since she was a little kid, she's always looked on the dark side of things. But in this case, she's probably right. I know I wouldn't hire either of them to work for me—too glum and timid."

He shook off the thought and turned to Nancy. "Want to take a walk with me in the garden?" he asked. "It's a beautiful evening."

"Actually," Nancy replied, "I was hoping to get a chance to talk with Nila alone. I want to ask her some questions before I speak to your father."

"Okay, Detective," he said with an impish grin. "What are you up to? Are you going to try and talk Father out of disowning us?"

"Never mind that," Nancy told him in a playful manner. "Do you know where Nila is, or don't you?"

"Of course I do," he said cheerfully. "Every

day at this time she takes a walk in the rose garden out back. You'll find her there. But I'm warning you, you'll have a better time with me than with the ice queen."

Nancy responded with a smile. "You're probably right. But I'm on the job, remember." With a wave, she headed outside for the back of the house.

As Philip had said, Nancy found Nila in the rose garden. "Ah, Nancy," Nila said when she spotted her coming. "Come here and smell these."

Nancy did as Nila requested. "Mmmm . . ." she said. "They really are amazing."

Looking at Nila out here, Nancy noticed the classical beauty of her features, and also a peace and lightness she hadn't seen before. It was as if a great weight had been lifted from Nila's shoulders. Nancy wondered if Pierce had told her about the new will.

"Nila," Nancy began cautiously, "could I ask you something?"

"Of course, Nancy," Nila said, turning her innocent, light blue eyes on Nancy. "What is it?"

"It's about the job you had before you came here," Nancy said. "I happened to hear about an article in a local newspaper. It was about you stealing from your former employer."

The question was packed with dynamite, and Nancy knew it. Nila blinked rapidly, and her delicate mouth widened in shock. "If the article said I stole anything, it's nothing but a pack of lies," she said firmly. "Show it to me!"

"I, er, I haven't even seen it, actually," Nancy admitted.

"Aha! I thought not! More poisoning of my reputation by Charles's family. I'm sure there is no such article. And if my former employer hadn't died, I would still be with her, and you could question her to your heart's content. She was a wonderful old lady, and I loved her dearly."

Her face softened, and Nancy suddenly felt sorry, even guilty, for bringing up the article without having first seen it.

"If you'll excuse me," Nancy said, backing away. "It's a little chilly out here. I'm going back inside." She'd found out what she'd come for. Now, Nancy wanted a few minutes alone to consider Nila's reaction, and her own next move.

"Of course," Nila said. "I'm sorry I snapped at you like that, Nancy. It's just that you have no idea what I've been put through since the day Charles's family showed up here."

"I'd like to hear more about that later," Nancy said, before heading back toward the house.

Nancy was confused. Nila had seemed so genuinely shocked and affronted when she'd been told about the article. It was impossible for Nancy to believe she was faking her surprise and indignation.

If Nila was innocent, then was she also innocent of faking the attempt on her life? That would fit in with the fact that someone had tried to kill Nancy. It would also mean that Nila still might be in danger. . . .

Nancy stepped inside, feeling worried and anxious. She wanted to find Bess and talk things over with her.

Nancy was about to close the door behind her, when she heard a piercing scream from the garden. It was followed by the sound of something smashing to the ground!

"Nila!" she gasped in horror. "Oh, no—no!"

Chapter

Ten

NANCY QUICKLY RAN back outside. She was
going to head for the rose garden, but stopped
short just outside the door.

Nila was kneeling on the path, both hands
grasping her head. Frightened sobs racked her
body. Alongside her on the path were the shat-
tered remnants of a brick. When Nancy looked
up, she saw a gap in the masonry of a parapet
surrounding the roof, three stories above. That
had to be where the brick had fallen from.

The rear door of the house opened, and Karen
and Philip ran outside to see what had happened. When they saw Nila on her knees, they
stopped short, unsure how to react. Nancy noticed that neither of them offered to help.

Eleanor ran out behind her niece and nephew,
followed by Bess, who went straight to Nancy's
side. Above them, a second story window flew

open, and a frightened and concerned Cecilia leaned out.

Nancy went to Nila and knelt beside her. "Are you all right?" Nancy asked, helping her to her feet.

"Yes, I—I think so," Nila stammered. "That brick—it came out of nowhere! I was just so—so stunned. It couldn't have missed me by more than a foot!"

"And it's a good thing it did," Nancy said soberly, kicking the remnants of the brick around with her toe. "If it had hit you, it could have killed you."

"We really ought to have Father hire a mason to check that brickwork," Karen said to Philip as they stood there, looking up toward the balcony around the roof. "Ever since he got sick, the house has been falling apart."

Nancy was shocked by their insensitivity. But was their blatant indifference evidence of something more sinister? Bess's voice interrupted Nancy's thoughts.

"Here, let me help you inside," Bess offered, slipping a supporting arm around Nila and guiding her past Karen and Philip. They and Eleanor followed Bess and Nila inside.

Cecilia stared down at Nancy from the open window. "Why do you keep coming around here?" she asked bluntly. "Haven't you caused enough trouble already?" Without waiting for Nancy to answer, Cecilia drew back inside and lowered the window.

Left alone, Nancy stared up at the window and

the roof above it. All at once the bushes behind her parted. Out stepped Jack, holding a length of rope in one hand and a golf club in the other. He held her eyes locked in a steely stare as he slowly approached her.

Nancy stumbled backward, startled. Jack stopped and lowered his hands. Then, suddenly, a trace of a smile played on his lips. "Did you think I was going to kill you?" he asked.

"It crossed my mind, to be honest," Nancy admitted.

"You've certainly given me a motive, for all the trouble you've caused between Karen and me."

"You're the one who caused the trouble, Jack," Nancy said, holding her ground. "I didn't gamble away Karen's money. And it hadn't been my intention to tell her, but she asked me point-blank what I'd learned about you. Should I have kept the truth from her?"

"Her own brother didn't seem to have a problem with it," Jack growled.

"I'm not Philip," Nancy countered.

"No kidding," Jack said. Then he sighed, and his broad shoulders sagged. "I know," he said. "You're right. I'm not a perfect person, okay? But I do love Karen. I just wanted the restaurant to be a big success. I thought if I could make one big win, I could expand, open some new outlets, really make a splash. I can't help it if things didn't pan out. I was unlucky."

Nancy shook her head. "A lot of times, we

make our own luck, Jack," she said. "And you were playing a loser's game."

He gritted his teeth, blinking hard. "I suppose you're going to tell Karen it's my fault that the old man's cutting us out of his will, too," he said under his breath.

"No. I'm not even going to get into that with her," Nancy assured him. "Karen can draw her own conclusions." Then something occurred to her. "Who told you Mr. Pierce was changing his will?" she asked.

"We all know about it," he said cryptically. "Family secrets don't stay secret for long—at least not around here."

"I see," Nancy said. "Well, that certainly gives you all a motive to kill Nila."

"Nobody's trying to kill Nila," he insisted. "And this rope proves it! I just found it in the bushes a minute ago."

He handed Nancy the rope. She could see that it was looped and knotted at one end, so that a brick would have fit just inside the loop. "You say you found this in the bushes?" she asked him warily.

"That's right. The way I see it, Nila had it all rigged. All she had to do was pull, then step back while the brick fell from the roof. Then she screams, tosses the rope in the bushes, and waits for everyone to show up." Jack flashed a nasty smile at her. "But then, you're so quick, you've probably figured all that out for yourself already."

91

Nancy narrowed her eyes. "And how did you happen to come by and find the rope she'd hidden in the bushes, if you don't mind my asking?"

"Not at all," Jack responded. "I'd been hitting plastic golf balls and lost one of them by the wall of the house. So I went behind the bushes to look for it. The rope nearly hit me on the head when she tossed it in." He showed her the golf ball in his palm.

"I see," Nancy said noncommittally. "Are you sure she threw the rope into the bushes? It couldn't have fallen from the roof?"

"Hmmm, I suppose it could have," Jack admitted. "But if someone was really trying to kill her, why not just throw the brick? Why bother with the rope?"

"Why indeed?" Nancy agreed. "Unless the person wanted to make it look like Nila was faking the whole thing."

Jack shrugged. "You're the detective," he said, his cold blue eyes fastened on her. "But I'll tell you one thing—*I* didn't try to kill her. I couldn't have gotten down here that fast from the roof, anyway."

Nancy fingered the rope in her hands. "Unless you had the rope all rigged beforehand and just yanked on it when she walked by," she pointed out, silencing him effectively. She walked toward the front of the house, leaving him there steaming.

After placing the rope in the trunk of her car,

Nancy headed back inside, thinking about Jack and the rest of Charles Pierce's family. With all those riches, they'd still managed to make themselves miserable. She hoped that, if they did inherit the old man's money, they'd handle it more wisely than they'd handled their previous fortunes.

Supper that night was a gloomy affair in the Pierce household. Nancy couldn't help thinking back to the engagement party, when the house had seemed so joyful. What a contrast! Too bad Bess hadn't gotten to see it then.

Charles Pierce didn't even come downstairs to join them. Eventually Jarvis the butler came in to say that Mr. Pierce was feeling tired after his long session with Mr. Bishop that afternoon and was going to have dinner in his room.

Turning to Nancy and Bess, Jarvis told them that Mr. Pierce had requested that they stay the night, and "conduct their business" first thing in the morning, before breakfast.

Nancy looked at Bess, whose eyes were bright with eager anticipation. "All right," Nancy told Jarvis. "We'll call our parents, but I'm sure it won't be a problem."

"Yes!" Bess whispered under her breath.

"Mr. Pierce wishes to see all of you at breakfast," Jarvis told the family members before departing. "There is something he'd like to announce."

With that, he headed for the kitchen, leaving a

heavy feeling of dread behind. Ominous, Nancy thought. Even dangerous. Everyone was sneaking silent glances at everyone else. Nila tried making a few casual remarks about the weather, but nobody replied. Not even Philip.

As soon as the meal was over, Nila said she wanted to check on Charles. The mood did not improve after she left. The rest of them sat around for another half hour, quietly eating dessert. Then Eleanor and Cecilia excused themselves, saying they were tired and wanted to get to bed early.

When they had gone, Philip turned to the others, and to Nancy's surprise, smiled mischievously. "Well," he said, "I think it's time we had a frank little talk."

Karen raised her eyebrows. "What's there to talk about, Phil?" she asked. "It's over. The ice queen has won. Nila's going to get all Dad's money, and we're all going to have to get regular jobs and work for a living like everyone else. I suppose there are worse fates. In fact," she concluded, looking meaningfully at her husband, "it might be just the thing for some of us."

"Hey, don't start on that again," Jack warned her.

"Oh, stop it, the two of you!" Philip broke in. "No fighting in front of our guests. Besides, we family members have to stick together if we're going to salvage anything out of this. First of all,

I think it's time to start mending fences with our new stepmother-to-be."

"Ugh," Karen said, making a face. "I'll never be able to be nice to her," she said.

"Well, try at least," Philip insisted.

"I don't know why you're all acting so blasé," Jack said bitterly.

"Look, Jack, nothing terrible's going to happen," Philip assured him, letting out an exasperated sigh. "Nila may hate us, but Dad certainly isn't going to let her cut us off completely. I'll be able to stay here and collect an allowance, and you can go on working for the company, at least for a while. As long as Dad's around, we won't be totally rejected."

"And how long do you think that's going to be, you idiot!" Jack shouted, slamming his fist on the table and rising to his feet. "As soon as that will's official, I wouldn't give you two cents for your father's life!"

Jack was clearly furious, and Nancy had to wonder if he had a point.

"Just what are you suggesting, Jack?" Karen asked.

"You know exactly what I mean," he retorted. "And don't pretend it hasn't occurred to you, too. Once she's in the will, she doesn't need him anymore. In fact, it will be better for her if he's out of the way. You're all acting so naive!" Throwing down his napkin, Jack stormed out of the dining room.

"Jack, wait!" Karen called, and quickly ran after him. "Let's not fight anymore."

Philip shook his head. "They've been at it for the past couple of hours," he said with a crooked smile. "Ah, married bliss."

"I'm afraid I had something to do with them fighting," Nancy said.

Philip shrugged. "It had to happen sooner or later," he said. "It's better this way. Maybe now Jack will face up to things and stop being such a jerk to Karen. Who knows, it may be the best thing that ever happened to that marriage."

"I'm relieved to hear you say that," Nancy said. "I was feeling kind of guilty."

"Aw, cheer up," he said, patting her shoulder affectionately. "Say, how would you two girls like to hear some really hot new CDs? The sound system I've got set up downstairs is totally awesome. Anyway, I think we could use a little distraction from all the gloom and doom around here. A little dancing might be just the thing."

"Sounds great to me," Nancy said. "Bess?"

"Great idea, Philip," Bess said, finishing her dish of sorbet and getting up. "Lead the way."

He guided them out through the kitchen and down the back stairs to the basement level, where an enormous space had been created for Philip's personal use. "Make yourselves at home down here," he told Nancy and Bess. "I've got to go up to my room and get the CDs. I was listening to them last night in bed."

Nancy and Bess used the time to call home and explore. There were billiard and Ping-Pong tables, and a parquet dance floor, complete with lighting effects available at the push of a button. They were just beginning to wonder what happened to Philip when he showed up, carrying a handful of disks. "Wait till you hear the sound quality down here," he said enthusiastically.

Nancy marveled at how easily he shrugged off the evening's worries. Maybe Philip had the right idea, she thought, as he twirled her onto the dance floor. Maybe if she stopped concentrating so hard on the case, some answers might just come to her. She let herself give in to the steady pulse of the music.

As they danced, with Bess playing with the high-tech equalizer controls, Nancy again felt a strong attraction for Philip Pierce.

"Tell me something," he said to Nancy as they took a break while Bess removed the CD from the deck. "Would you have gone out with me if you'd known I'd be flat broke in a week?"

Nancy took his hand, looking him straight in the eye. "I didn't go out with you because you were rich," she said.

"Ah. You wanted to investigate me," he remembered.

Nancy shook her head. "That's not why, either."

"I'd better open the window," Philip said as he released her. "It's getting warm in here."

He reached up and opened the basement window. As soon as he did, they heard an unmistakable sound. A scream. Nila's scream! Then another and another and another . . .

The basement door flew open and Cecilia was standing there. "Come quickly!" she told them. "I think something's happened to Uncle Charles!"

Chapter
Eleven

THEY CHARGED UP THE STAIRS to the second floor and down the hallway to Charles Pierce's suite. Eleanor was running toward the room from the other direction, and Karen and Jack were at the doorway.

"It's the old man," Jack told them, his face reflecting his concern and rage. "I think he's dead."

Nancy rushed past him into the suite. She found Nila sitting on the edge of the bed, sobbing as she embraced Charles Pierce, who lay unconscious in bed, his face white as chalk.

Nancy didn't waste time asking the distraught Nila questions. Instead, she felt for Pierce's pulse and was relieved to find that he was still alive. The heartbeat was weak and uneven but still there. "Bess, call an ambulance!" she shouted. Her friend ran to the nearest phone.

"It's his heart," Nila managed to say between sobs. Either she was the best actress Nancy had ever seen or she was truly, deeply upset. "I came in to give him his medicine, and I found him like this."

Nancy saw the bottle of pills and the nearly empty glass of water on the bedside table. As Nancy got up to examine them, Karen walked over to her father and took his hand in hers. Tears trickled down her cheeks. "Oh, Daddy," she said in a small voice. "Please don't die. Please don't die."

Philip came up behind his sister and put his arms around her. "He'll pull through," he said. "He's a tough old bird."

"There's so much I still want to tell him," Karen said tearfully. Philip just squeezed her shoulders tighter and nodded. Nancy was touched by their sorrow and surprised by it, too. She'd never suspected how much the two Pierce children actually cared for their father. He hadn't been around very much while they were growing up, and Philip had even told her he didn't much like his dad. Judging by the expression on his face, even he hadn't been aware of how deeply he cared for his father—until now.

The sound of ambulance sirens broke into Nancy's thoughts. Soon the emergency medical team had bundled Pierce onto a stretcher and carried him out of the house. The whole family got into cars and followed the ambulance to the hospital. Nancy and Bess went along, too. Nancy wanted to make sure this sudden medical crisis had natural causes.

They all took seats in the waiting room outside the intensive care unit. Nancy leaned against a wall, watching the others.

Jack paced while Eleanor comforted Cecilia, and Philip did the same for his sister. Bess sat with Nila, trying to keep her from hopping up and arguing with the staff that she should be allowed inside with her future husband. After all, she kept saying, she was a nurse herself. They finally did let her in to see him briefly, after they had stabilized his vital signs and finished examining him.

But there was nothing Nila or any of them could do for Pierce right then—nothing but wait. It was two hours before the doctor in charge stepped into the waiting room, his face impassive and serious.

"There's been no change in Mr. Pierce's condition," he told them. "He's alive but comatose. He may or may not make it through this. His condition is stable for the moment, though. We'll have to wait and see.

"For now, it's very late, and I suggest you all go home and get some sleep. Call in the morning, and we'll update you."

"But I want to stay with him," Nila cried.

The doctor shook his head. "You need to rest, ma'am," he said. "You've had quite a shock, and you can't do him any good if you haven't had any sleep. I assure you, if there's the least change in his condition, we'll call you immediately."

101

Reluctantly Nila consented to go. They all filed out of the hospital, acknowledging their exhaustion and the futility of waiting around any longer.

None of them said much as they rode the elevator down to the lobby. Clearly, everyone was worried. Nancy studied them all carefully. She hated thinking it, but she had to wonder which they were more worried about—Pierce dying, or being left out of his will if he did.

None of them, except Nancy and Bess, knew that the will hadn't been signed already. As far as the heirs were concerned, the deed had already been done.

One by one, they all said good night and went to bed. Jarvis showed Nancy and Bess to their room, and soon Nancy found herself drifting off into a troubled, dream-filled sleep.

They all gathered over a somber breakfast the next morning. Karen asked Jarvis to bring her a cordless phone, and she dialed the hospital. Everyone watched her silently as she waited for the doctor to come on the line.

"Hello— Yes . . . Oh, thank goodness!" Turning to the rest of them, she whispered, "There's been no change." Then, she turned her attention back to the phone. "Oh . . . I see . . . but it is possible he'll recover fully, isn't it? Isn't it?" Her face fell as she listened. She turned to the others and in a halting, croaking voice she said, "The doctor says if he lives, he'll probably have severe brain damage."

An audible gasp rippled through the room at the awful news. But Karen's attention was suddenly riveted back to the phone. "What? I don't understand. Yes, but—no! You can't be serious!" Her face drained of color as she stared at Nila and slowly hung up the phone.

"What is it?" Jack asked, springing up and going over to her.

"It wasn't a heart attack after all," Karen told them, her eyes wide and blinking rapidly. "It was an overdose of Father's medicine. It slowed his metabolism down so much that his brain was starved for oxygen, and he went into a coma. The doctor says he's calling in the police."

"You," Philip shouted, pointing at Nila, who had shrunk back in her chair, thunderstruck. "You poisoned him!"

He moved forward, but Nancy stopped him. "Just hold on a minute!" she ordered. "Let's not accuse anyone of anything. None of us knows what happened."

"Of course we do," Cecilia suddenly piped up. She seemed extremely agitated and upset. "Nila always gives Uncle Charles his medicine."

Eleanor bit her lip, her eyes shifting nervously. "It's true," she agreed. "And we're all aware that Charles met with Mr. Bishop yesterday."

"Of course," Jack broke in, furious. "Isn't it obvious what's happened? As soon as she knew the money was hers, she tried to get rid of him."

"Stop it!" Nila screamed, covering both ears with her hands. "Stop it, all of you! I didn't give Charles his medicine last night. I already told

103

you, he was unconscious when I went into the room!"

Nancy and Bess exchanged glances. Nancy frowned, remembering the nearly empty water glass and the open bottle of pills by Pierce's bedside. Clearly, he had taken the pills. Was Nila lying? Or was there another explanation?

Pierce could have taken the overdose of pills himself, but Nancy didn't think that a likely possibility—a man in love and about to get married didn't kill himself deliberately. Nor could it have been an accident. Not with Nila keeping track of everything.

No, there were only two likely explanations. Either Nila had done what the others were accusing her of, or someone else had done it—someone who had repeatedly tried and failed to kill Nila, and who was now trying to kill Pierce and frame her for his murder.

For an awful moment Nancy remembered how long she and Bess waited for Philip to return to the basement rec room the night before. But picturing Philip's stricken face at his father's bedside made her dismiss the idea. At least for now.

Just then Mr. Bishop, Pierce's lawyer, was ushered in by the butler. "I heard the news this morning and got over here as fast as I could," he told them. "It's already on the radio about Mr. Pierce's heart attack."

"Tell me, Mr. Bishop," Jack said, staring at Nila. "Can a murderer inherit money from her victim?"

"Why, no," Bishop said, taken aback. "Why do you ask?"

"Because," Nila interrupted, "he thinks I tried to kill Charles. They all think so. But it isn't true! I love Charles. No," she said, staring at them all in cold fury, "one of you has been trying to kill me, and now you've tried to kill Charles. But you're too late. Even if he dies, you won't get his money. He made a new will yesterday, leaving everything to me! Isn't that right, Mr. Bishop?"

Bishop went red in the face. "I . . . er . . . I'm not supposed to say," he stammered. "In fact, I was supposed to come over here this morning to pick up the signed copies. I left them here yesterday for Mr. Pierce to sign and have witnessed."

Nancy and Bess exchanged glances. None of the others knew what they knew—that the will had never been signed. But Nancy decided not to say anything. She wanted to watch the way everyone behaved. She knew that when people were upset, they often let things slip.

"Jarvis," Mr. Bishop said, "would you mind going to Mr. Pierce's study and fetching the copies of the new will for us?"

"Certainly, Mr. Bishop," the butler said, and left the room.

Nancy couldn't take her eyes off Nila. Her face had changed completely, from that of a grieving wife-to-be to a mask of cold, bitter fury. Her ice-blue eyes challenged everyone in the room.

Nancy tried to think through the events of the last twelve hours. Had Nila given Pierce the overdose? She certainly had a strong motive, assuming she thought the will had already been signed.

Of course, if Pierce pulled through and regained full mental capacity, he'd be able to identify whoever had administered the overdose. But as the doctor had said, that didn't seem likely. And as a nurse, Nila would have been well aware of what constituted a lethal dose.

Suddenly they all heard running footsteps. The butler ran into the room, gasping for breath. "Oh, Mr. Bishop!" he said fearfully. "Mr. Bishop—the copies of the new will—they're gone! They've disappeared!"

Chapter

Twelve

A CHORUS OF GASPS broke out in the room, followed by an anguished cry from Nila, who sank down into her chair. Nancy quickly looked around at the members of Charles Pierce's family. Not surprisingly, every one of them seemed relieved, except for Eleanor, Nancy noted. Charles Pierce's widowed sister-in-law was acting distinctly worried, and Nancy wondered why.

"What happens now, Mr. Bishop?" Cecilia asked.

"Well," he said with a sigh, "if Mr. Pierce should die or become incapacitated, his most recent will would take precedence. That means, if the new will can't be found, the old will would still be in effect."

Nancy listened closely. Until this moment there had been two possibilities. Now, there was only one. In any investigation, Nancy knew, the detective needed to look at who benefited from the crime. In this case, the answer was: everyone *but* Nila. Therefore, it no longer made sense that Nila faked the attempts on her life, then tried to kill Pierce after he changed his will.

Nancy's thoughts ran backward over the various attempts on Nila's life. One piece still didn't fit—the lab report on Nila's glass of cranberry juice.

Nancy pictured the scene, hoping to jog her memory for a clue. She remembered Eleanor standing there in the hallway, over Nila's body, a glass in her hand. . . .

"Of course!" she cried out loud.

"Excuse me?" Karen said, turning toward her.

"No, excuse *me,*" Nancy replied. "Bess and I have to be going now. We'll be back later. I hope you find the will, Mr. Bishop. 'Bye, everyone."

Before any of them could react, Nancy had yanked Bess's arm, and the two of them were driving back toward the center of town.

"What was that all about?" Bess asked, confused. "Why did we need to get out of there in such a hurry?"

"We've got things to do," Nancy answered as she drove. "First of all, my car should be ready by now. I don't need to drag you around with me on all my little errands."

"But I want to come," Bess protested. "This is all so fascinating. I can't wait to tell George all about—"

"Here we are," Nancy interrupted, pulling into the garage. It took her only a few minutes to pick up her car and pay the bill. "Bess, I've got to go now," she told her friend. Before Bess could protest, she added, "I'll call you later after I've cleared up a few things."

Bess opened her mouth to say something, but Nancy stopped her with a quick kiss on the cheek. "I'll explain everything later," she said hurriedly, making for her car. "Gotta run!"

Nancy took off for home, glad to be behind the wheel of her Mustang once more. It was her pride and joy, and it really steamed her that someone had tampered with it. She was determined to put that person behind bars—for her own sake, as well as Charles Pierce's and Nila's.

At home she raced upstairs to her room and started pulling clothes out of her laundry hamper. "Ah! Here it is!" she said triumphantly, holding up the dress she'd worn to the engagement party. "Good thing I was in too much of a hurry to take care of this stain."

There it was, a blotch of dark red. Going over to her bedside phone, she called her friend at the police lab again.

"Sorry to bother you, Ernie," she said. "But could you run another test for me? Same one as last time?"

"I don't know, Nan," Ernie said. "We're really busy around here. If my boss finds out, he'll kill me."

"I'll take full responsibility," Nancy assured

him. "You can blame it all on me. Tell him you're helping me catch an attempted murderer."

"Whoa," Ernie said, impressed. "I guess you didn't like the way the last test came out, huh?"

"Things have changed since then," Nancy told him. "I've got a feeling the criminal's been one step ahead of me—until now."

Nancy's next stop was the main branch of the River Heights Public Library, where she proceeded to go over microfilmed back issues of the Stockton *Gazette* until she came to the one she was looking for.

There was the article, all right. Except that the photograph in it wasn't of Nila Kirkedottir at all! The woman pictured had dark hair and horn-rimmed glasses, and the article identified her as Ellen Ramsbottom. Nancy noted that both names, Ellen Ramsbottom and Nila Kirkedottir, were of about equal length. The forger would have had to substitute one name for the other, finding a similar type font, and then simply switch a photo of Nila for one of the guilty nurse.

That is, if there had even been an altered article. Nancy only had Eleanor's word for it. Eleanor, who'd been there in the hallway, standing over Nila. Eleanor, who'd known Nancy was a detective before anyone else did. Eleanor, who'd eavesdropped on her conversation with Pierce and knew he'd drafted a new will. . . .

Nancy ran off a copy of the article and left the library, heading straight for the Pierce mansion.

She'd been gone for only a few hours, but in that time, the butler told her, Philip, Jack, and Karen had all gone out. Mr. Bishop had also left. Nila had gone to bed, as had Cecilia.

Well, they'd all had a long and stressful night, Nancy thought, although she herself was too wired to feel the least bit sleepy. "Where's Eleanor?" she asked the butler.

"I believe she's in the garden, miss," the butler informed her.

Nancy thanked him and went around to the back of the house. She found Eleanor seated in the gazebo, appearing even more troubled than she had earlier in the morning.

Nancy sat down beside her and gave her a little smile. "Well," she began. "You must feel pretty relieved, huh?"

Eleanor stared at her, uncomprehending. "Wh-what do you mean?" she asked.

"Well, the will, of course," Nancy said, shrugging. "I mean, the new one. It's gone, so you and Philip and Karen will all inherit your fair share. Right?"

"Oh. I see what you mean," Eleanor said with an anxious sigh. "Yes, I suppose that's true. But poor Charles."

"Is that what you're so worried about?" Nancy asked her pointedly.

"Oh. Do I seem worried? Yes, I suppose that's why," Eleanor replied, forcing a smile.

"Mmmm," Nancy said, nodding. "Are you sure it isn't because you're afraid I'll find out the truth?"

Eleanor's face suddenly lost what little color it had. "The truth?" she said, her voice faltering. "I—I don't know what you mean. . . ."

"I mean this for starters," Nancy said sternly, whipping out the article and showing it to her.

"Oh!" Eleanor gasped when she saw the picture. "But—but that's not Nila at all. The copy I saw had her name and picture on it."

"I think," Nancy said, noting that Eleanor's surprise seemed genuine, "that it's time you told me who showed you that article."

Eleanor glanced up at her, biting her lip. "It—it was Jack," she admitted. "Jack showed it to me one night when he and Karen had Cecilia and me over to dinner."

"All right," Nancy said, getting up. "Let's go on over there and have a little talk with Jack. We're going to get to the bottom of this—right now."

No one answered the doorbell at Jack and Karen's house. No one except two dogs, who yapped loudly from inside. "I have the key, though," Eleanor told Nancy, taking it out of her purse. "Cecilia and I feed their dogs whenever they go on vacation, you see." She fitted the key into the lock, and she and Nancy went inside.

Nancy spoke soothingly to the excited Lhasa apsos, while Eleanor glanced around the room. "I'm pretty sure where Jack has the article," Eleanor told Nancy. "I saw him take it out of a wooden box he keeps on his desk."

She led Nancy into Jack's wood-paneled office,

which was so cluttered it was hard to find a way to the desk. Jack, it seemed, was not organized.

Nancy picked up the wooden box that lay on top of the desk, covered by papers and magazines. Sure enough, the copy of the article was inside—with *Nila's* picture and name on it.

So Eleanor had been telling the truth, Nancy realized. Jack really had shown her the article, and her surprise when Nancy showed her the real copy had been genuine.

Suddenly Nancy's suspicions focused on Jack. He had a temper; he had criminal associations; and he had gambled away his wife's inheritance. Mr. Pierce had even suggested Jack had married Karen only for her money. He hated Nila and certainly had the opportunity to make the attempts on her life.

Nancy looked around his office, her practiced eyes searching for any clue.

There were all sorts of notices from creditors, threatening him unless he paid what he owed them. Clearly Jack was in big-league financial trouble and desperately needed the money Pierce would leave Karen. Did that mean he would try to commit murder, though?

Nancy's eyes went to the wastebasket at the side of the desk where Eleanor stood. It was filled with crumpled papers. Nancy bent down to examine them, and that was when she saw it.

The greasy rag had caught on the side of the wicker basket. Odd that such a dirty item would find its way into an office.

Nancy gasped. There were greasy fingerprints

113

all over the rag. Were they the fingerprints of the person who'd tried to sabotage her car?

"That's funny," Eleanor said, seeing the rag in Nancy's hands. "Jack never fixes his own car. . . ."

"Hey!" Jack's voice came from the doorway, freezing both women where they stood. "What are you two doing in here?"

His voice was angry, but his face was even angrier—murderously angry.

Chapter
Thirteen

W HAT ARE YOU TWO DOING HERE?" he repeated, a threatening tone in his voice. "Who told you you could snoop around like this?"

"Now, Jack," Eleanor said in a quavering voice, holding out a restraining hand toward him, "I just wanted to show Nancy that article about Nila stealing from that poor old woman, and I remembered it was here, in that box on your desk," she finished, her voice tapering off to a mere whisper. "I did have the key you gave me—so I—we—um . . ."

Jack grunted huffily, but the explanation Eleanor had given him—that they were investigating Nila, not him—mollified him a bit. "Well, I see you found what you were looking for," he said, eyeing the article in Nancy's hand. "Now get out. You can take it with you, but don't ever let me catch you sneaking into my house again, understand?"

"Of course not, Jack," Eleanor assured him.

"And give me back my key while you're at it," he said, grabbing it out of her hand roughly.

"Just a moment, Jack," Nancy broke in. "Not so fast. There are one or two things that I need to clear up with you."

"I don't have to talk to you," he reminded her. "You're not a cop, and I haven't done anything wrong."

"Maybe not," Nancy replied, "but the police will be wanting to talk to you soon. I happen to have a lot of friends on the force, and I'll be telling them all about my investigation. It might go very hard on you if I tell them everything I've found out."

Jack seemed torn between the urge to rip her apart right there and his anxiety over what she might know about him. "All right," he said finally, sinking down into the swivel chair behind his desk. "What do you want to know?"

"First of all," Nancy began, brushing aside a few of the papers on top of the desk and perching herself on the cleared spot, "it was you who asked Tom Walczek to steal the draft of Mr. Pierce's new will, wasn't it?"

Jack clenched his jaw so tightly Nancy was afraid he'd break his teeth. "Yeah, that was me," he said. "It was pretty stupid, but I had to know what was in it. Anyway, it doesn't mean I tried to kill anybody, because I didn't."

"All right," Nancy said. "Second of all, this copy of the article about Nila is a forgery."

"What?" Jack's eyes widened, and he stared at Eleanor, seemingly flabbergasted.

"We should go now, Nancy," Eleanor said, sounding nervous. "Cecilia will wonder where I am."

"I looked up the real article at the library," Nancy told Jack, ignoring Eleanor. "The photograph and the name have been changed. The nurse who stole from her employer wasn't Nila at all."

"B-but—" Jack sputtered.

"So you see," Nancy continued, "someone's been out to get Nila all along. I was just wondering if it might be you."

Jack bolted up out of his chair, slamming both palms down on the desktop. "Don't you start accusing me," he bellowed. "It wasn't me who fooled with that article. If you're looking for a criminal, try her!" he said, pointing to Eleanor, who shrank back in terror. "She's the one who showed me the article."

"What?" Nancy asked, taken aback. "But, Eleanor, you said—"

"N-no, Jack," Eleanor said, standing her ground with her back against the office door. "Don't you remember? You showed it to me, not the other way around."

"She's lying!" Jack shouted, pointing at her. "Look at her—can't you see she's lying?"

Nancy bit her lip, thinking fast. Eleanor was

less likely to be lying than Jack, she decided. He was probably much more practiced at it. "Eleanor," she said, "would you mind waiting for me outside? I'd like to talk to Jack for a moment."

Eleanor put a hand to her mouth. "Are you sure you'll be all right?" she asked. "Maybe you should come, too."

"I'll be fine," Nancy assured her. "Go on ahead. I'll be right out."

Eleanor nodded reluctantly and backed out of the room, slowly shutting the door behind her.

Jack put a finger to his lips and walked past Nancy to the door. He yanked it open, peeked out into the hallway, then shut it again. "Just a precaution," he said. "She listens at doors."

"Yes, I know," Nancy said with a sigh.

"So," he said, still standing in front of the door, blocking Nancy's exit, "where were we?"

"You were saying it was Eleanor who showed you the article?"

"Yes. She told me someone had shown it to her, but she wouldn't say who. Now she's saying *I* showed it to her—ha! She's got some nerve, you know? What a manipulator! You'd never think a timid little mouse like her would have the gall."

"There's something else I want to ask you about," Nancy said, holding up the greasy rag. "What was this doing in your office waste-basket?"

Jack took the rag from her and examined it. "Never seen it before," he said. "Feels like car grease."

"It is," Nancy agreed. "The night before last, someone sabotaged my car. I nearly smashed into a telephone pole. I could have been killed. In fact, I think that was the plan."

Jack looked at her for a long moment. "I see," he said. "And you say you found this here? In my wastebasket?"

"Just now," Nancy replied. "Of course, the grease could have come from any car. But you must admit it looks kind of suspicious. I mean, it's not the kind of thing that usually winds up in someone's office waste basket."

Jack blew out a breath of air and rolled his eyes. "But don't you see?" he said. "She planted it there! Isn't it obvious? She drags you over here to get the article she showed me—tells you *I* showed it to *her*—then plants this rag in my trash so you can find it. She's setting me up, Nancy! Can't you see that?"

"Maybe," Nancy said noncommittally. "Or maybe you're just plain guilty. Either way, I'm going to find out, Jack."

"Hey!" Jack said suddenly, snapping his fingers. "Two nights ago—that was right before you caught me with the suitcase, right?"

"Right."

"Well, then, I've got an ironclad alibi, Miss Hot-Shot Detective. It so happens I spent that whole night at Tom's gambling establishment. He wasn't there, but you can ask him to check with his staff if you don't believe me. Here, I'll dial the number for you." He proceeded to do just that.

"Jack," Nancy cautioned him. "Tom's staff may not exactly be what I'd call reliable witnesses."

"Okay, okay," Jack said, waiting for someone to pick up on the other end of the phone line. "But there have to be twenty guys who can place me there that night. Hey, I'm not proud I was there, but I'm no murderer. Hello? This is Jack Oliver. Let me speak to Tom," he said into the phone.

Nancy waited until Tom came on the line and Jack explained things to him. Satisfied with the response, Jack handed Nancy the phone. Sure enough, Tom told her that some of his staff could confirm that Jack had been there the entire night in question. For what it was worth, Jack did indeed have an alibi.

"I'm going to make a list of everyone I know who was there that night," Jack told Nancy as he hung up. "No way I'm going to take the rap for trying to kill *you!*"

Nancy left him then and went outside, where Eleanor was waiting for her. The two of them got into Nancy's car and drove back toward the mansion.

"Eleanor," Nancy began gently as they drove past the downtown area, "you still insist it was Jack who showed you that article?"

Eleanor flushed momentarily. "Why, yes," she said.

"So you're saying he's lying? That he's the forger?"

"I'm not saying anything of the kind," Eleanor

said quickly. "And I'm not going to, either. I'm not going to accuse anyone of anything."

Nancy held her tongue, well aware that she couldn't bully the truth out of Eleanor—not yet, anyway. She dropped off the flustered woman, then headed back home, where she called her friend at the police lab.

"Ernie?" she asked. "What have you got for me?"

"I don't know how you know these things, Drew," Ernie said admiringly. "But sure enough, this test came up positive."

"Positive?" Nancy repeated, excited that the last piece of the puzzle clearing Nila was now falling into place.

"Yep," Ernie said. "It was cranberry juice again, but this time it was heavily laced with rat poison!"

Chapter

Fourteen

RAT POISON!

Nancy hung up the phone slowly. Several emotions washed over her—triumph, confusion, sadness, all jumbled together. She remembered vividly the image of Eleanor that first night, kneeling over Nila's unconscious form, one empty glass tipped over on the carpet, another in Eleanor's hand. How quick it would have been for her to switch those glasses—a matter of seconds!

Other images crossed Nancy's mind. The sneaky way Eleanor had disposed of the rat poison. After all, rat poison was a common household item, and no one at the time had suggested it was the cause of Nila's illness the night before. Why should Eleanor have looked so furtive, so guilty, about throwing it away?

Eleanor hiding after listening in on Nancy's

private conversation with Pierce. Eleanor, who knew Nancy was a detective before any of the others.

And it was Eleanor, Nancy remembered, who'd told her about the newspaper article, who'd led her to Jack's house, where they'd found it, and who'd been standing next to the wastebasket where Nancy had found the greasy rag . . .

The pieces were certainly beginning to fall into place. And yet, Nancy didn't feel entirely happy about it. Eleanor Pierce did not seem to be the sort of person who had it in her to kill. Cunning, yes—the eavesdropping proved that, as did the clever withholding of information, only to drop it in dribs and drabs as the occasion suited her.

But it was hard for Nancy to imagine Eleanor getting down on her knees with a wrench and loosening the bolts on her car wheel; or up on the roof of the mansion, throwing a brick down at Nila's head; or administering a potentially fatal overdose to her brother-in-law, who'd taken her in and been so kind to her for years.

Eleanor didn't seem like a cruel person or an evil person. Of course, Nancy knew from personal experience that murderers didn't always fit the stereotype of a killer. Still, she was bothered.

Frowning, she sat back down on the edge of her bed and dialed Bess's number.

"I thought you'd never call," Bess complained. "I've been sitting around here all day waiting, do you realize that? What's been going on?"

"A lot," Nancy told her. "Do you think you could get over here right away? We have to talk."

While she waited for Bess, Nancy played back her messages. One was from Sergeant O'Rourke at homicide. "Hello, Nancy," his deep voice boomed. "I'm over at the Pierce mansion, and I understand you've been doing some investigating for Mr. Pierce this week. Knowing you, I'm sure you're well aware what's been going on. I've been interviewing the family members and staff, and I'll be wanting to talk to you before I make an arrest. So, please, when you get this message, give me a buzz, or just head on down to headquarters, all right? Thanks."

Nancy sighed, debating what to do. She knew that when O'Rourke referred to making an arrest, he meant Nila Kirkedottir. She was the one who regularly gave Charles Pierce his nighttime medication, and she would be his number one suspect. Nancy felt sorry for Nila. After all she'd been through, a police grilling was the last thing she needed.

Nancy knew that if she couldn't crack the case in the next twenty-four hours, she'd have to turn things over to O'Rourke and the River Heights Police Department. She also knew that right now that would be counterproductive. She'd already learned so much on her own that she felt she'd come to know these people. And she was so close—she could feel the solution just beyond her grasp!

Twenty-four hours, she promised herself. If she hadn't wrapped up things by then, she'd march over to police headquarters and turn things over to O'Rourke. Until then she'd just forget she'd played back her messages.

Bess arrived, flushed and out of breath. She had obviously raced over. "So dish, Drew," she said, as Nancy answered the door and led her into the kitchen for a snack. "What did I miss?"

"I've got to break this case wide open, Bess," Nancy replied, "and I've got to do it in a hurry. The police are moving in, and they're going to take over if I don't wrap up things by tonight."

"But how can you do that?" Bess asked in astonishment. "You don't know who did it, do you?"

Nancy stopped in her tracks, snapping her fingers as the light bulb went off in her head. "Bess, you're a genius!" she cried.

"Gee, thanks," Bess chirped. "I've always thought so myself—"

"What you just said—it gave me a great idea. It's true, I don't know who's behind it all, but none of the suspects know that."

"I don't get you," Bess admitted, taking a cookie.

"Just listen," Nancy said, plopping down in a chair opposite her puzzled friend. "I'm going to do something really dramatic to crack this case. And you're going to help me."

"Oh, goodie," Bess said. "I love dramas."

"Now, here's the plan. . . ." Nancy began.

In response to Nancy's phone call, the butler had summoned all the family members together

125

in the parlor of the Pierce estate. The grandfather clock had just finished striking eight when Nancy walked in to face her suspects.

They were all there, waiting. Jack and Karen sat next to each other. He was holding her hand, although she looked uncomfortable, as if she would gladly free herself if he would loosen his grip.

Philip sat on the sofa, an arm draped around Cecilia, who was nervously picking at her cuticles. Philip gave Nancy a wink and a grin, which she acknowledged with a simple nod of her head. Now was not the time, she knew, to let his charm put her off balance.

On the other side of Cecilia sat Eleanor, fanning herself with her hand. Nancy noticed that the room was rather stuffy. All the windows were shut, and the silence was heavy in the dimly lit parlor.

Below the portrait of Pierce and his bride-to-be stood Nila, stock-still, coldly regarding the members of the Pierce family, one of whom had repeatedly tried to kill her and had now nearly killed her beloved Charles.

It was just like in the movies, Nancy reflected. But this was no movie. This was dangerously real.

"Hello, everyone," Nancy began as the butler shut the door behind her. "I want to thank you all for being here. I realize it's short notice, but as you know, the police have begun their investigation, so I think it's time I finish mine."

Out of the corner of her eye, Nancy thought

she caught the slightest sign of relief on Eleanor's haggard face.

"I want you all to know," Nancy continued, "that I know who tried to kill Charles Pierce. That same person also tried to kill me and repeatedly tried to kill Nila Kirkedottir."

She nodded at Nila, who nodded back, with surprise and sudden admiration.

Around the room, audible gasps went up from the family.

"Well, who is it?" Philip asked, a cryptic smile playing across his lips. "Which one of us is the would-be murderer, Nancy? Because whoever it is certainly isn't very good at it. After all, no one's died yet, right?"

Nancy couldn't help herself. She had to smile back at him. "Not yet, thank goodness," she agreed. "As to which one of you it is, I don't want to say here and now. I just wanted you to know that I have positive proof of the criminal's identity, and I'm going to the police with it as soon as we're finished here. It will go easier if the person concerned cooperates fully and makes a full and prompt confession. That's all. Thanks again for coming."

There. She'd done what she'd come to do. Nancy turned and reached for the doorknob, hoping that somebody would try to stop her.

Somebody did. "Wait!" Eleanor shouted, suddenly leaping to her feet. "All right, you win!"

"Mother, no!" Cecilia screamed, grabbing Eleanor in a desperate bear hug. "Don't do this."

"Shut up, Eleanor," Jack warned her. "Can't

you see she's bluffing? Let her go to the police—
she's got nothing on you or any of us."

Eleanor wasn't listening, though. Clearly, she
believed Nancy. "You win," she repeated. "Take
me with you. I'm the one—I'm the one who was
behind it all!"

Chapter

Fifteen

"You can't be serious, Nancy!" Philip exclaimed. "Eleanor couldn't have done those things—any of them. Just one look at her ought to tell you that."

"Honestly," Karen agreed. "This whole thing is a farce. Eleanor, let me call Mr. Bishop. He'll straighten all this out—"

"I'm going with Nancy," Eleanor calmly informed them. "This has gone on long enough, and it's got to stop. I don't want the police arresting the wrong person. You're innocent, all of you. I've got to take responsibility for what I've done."

"But—" Philip stopped in midsentence, speechless.

"Mother, no!" Cecilia screamed, tugging at her mother as Eleanor turned toward the door. "Why are you doing this?"

"I'm sorry, darling," Eleanor told her, kissing Cecilia's forehead. "There's no other way out."

"But it's all a lie," Cecilia said, turning to Nancy. "She's innocent! Innocent!" Cecilia dissolved into tears, her body wracked with wrenching sobs as her mother, slipping gently from her grasp, followed Nancy out the door.

Nancy put an arm around Eleanor's shoulders and led her outside, while Philip and Jack restrained the hysterical Cecilia. The Mustang convertible waited at the bottom of the front steps, its motor running. Nancy opened the passenger door, flipped the front seat forward, and said, "Get in, Eleanor."

Bess was sitting behind the wheel. Eleanor seemed taken aback to see her there but climbed into the backseat dutifully. Nancy pushed the driver's seat back into position and climbed in beside Bess. "Okay, let's go," Nancy told her friend.

Bess started the car down the long driveway. Her jaw was hanging open in shock. "Eleanor?" she finally said. "Nan, there's got to be some mistake!"

"No, Bess," Nancy said. "There's no mistake. Eleanor's already confessed."

"Nan, Eleanor was not the one who threw the brick at Nila," Bess said. "Because I was with her in the house when it happened."

"What? Are you sure?"

"Sure I'm sure," Bess said. "We heard the scream, gave each other a look, and went running for the back door."

"Bess," Nancy scolded her. "Why didn't you tell me this before?"

"You didn't ask me!" Bess shot back.

Nancy looked back at the house. She could see the faces clustered at the parlor window, watching them depart. She knew she had to think fast. "Keep driving!" she ordered.

Bess turned onto the main road, and the house disappeared from view.

"Okay, now pull over," Nancy said. Bess quickly did as she was told.

"Why are we stopping?" Eleanor asked from the backseat. "What's going on?"

"The game's over, Eleanor," Nancy told her. "Who did you think you were fooling?"

"I—" An alarmed expression spread across Eleanor's face. "Oh, but that brick falling was probably just an accident."

"I don't think so," Nancy countered. "Look, Eleanor—we want the truth. *Now.*"

"I—I don't know what you're talking about. I . . ."

"All right, Bess," Nancy said, getting out of the car. "Take Eleanor for a nice, long drive. Keep her occupied for the next hour or so."

"Wait!" Eleanor shouted. "Where are you going?"

"Back to the house," Nancy informed her. "I was lying when I said I knew who the criminal was, but you *do* know, Eleanor. You've known all along. And now, I know, too."

"No—no!" Eleanor cried out.

131

"When you saw that Nila had swallowed rat poison," Nancy went on, "you switched glasses with her to throw me off the track. Then you tried to throw the rat poison away. Lucky for me I caught you at it. And now you're going so far as to give yourself up in order to save someone else."

"No!" Eleanor gasped. "No, you've got it all wrong."

"I don't think so," Nancy said. "In fact, I'm sure I'm right. Okay, Bess, drive on." Nancy shut the door and the Mustang took off.

Nancy turned back toward the Pierce mansion, walking purposefully and swiftly. Eleanor had been protecting someone. She might also have been hiding evidence. If so, the guilty party might now try to destroy that evidence. There was no time to lose.

Jack was alone in the parlor when Nancy got back inside.

"Back so soon?" he asked her. "Where's Eleanor?"

"Bess is driving her down to police headquarters," Nancy said, only half fibbing. "Where is everyone?"

Jack shrugged. "Cecilia ran off, hysterical. Karen went to call Bishop, to tell him about Eleanor's confession. As for Philip—who knows? Maybe he's romancing Nila. Phil's an opportunist—and it can't hurt to get close to a potential heiress, can it? Especially when the fortune she's going to inherit should have been his—"

Nancy shook her head in disgust and left Jack sitting there. She headed for the main staircase that led upstairs. If Eleanor had been hiding any evidence, it would probably be in her suite somewhere. Nancy hoped Eleanor had had the foresight to lock her door against intruders.

As she walked down the carpeted hallway toward the stairs, Nancy felt a chill go up her spine. It was quiet—too quiet. No Cecilia sobbing, no murmuring voices talking to lawyers on telephones—nothing.

"Nancy!"

She nearly jumped at the sound of Philip's voice just inches behind her.

"Oh, you startled me!" she gasped. "Don't ever do that again."

"Sneaking up on somebody, were you?" Philip asked. "I hope it wasn't me."

"No, I wasn't sneaking anywhere," Nancy replied. *"You* were sneaking up on *me."*

"Just to get a chance to kiss the back of your neck," Philip said with a smile.

"Not now, Philip," Nancy said. "I'm busy."

"With what?" he wanted to know. "I thought you were taking Eleanor down to police headquarters."

"Bess is doing that for me. I've got work to do."

"Work? But I thought the case was all wrapped up." He seemed genuinely puzzled and not a little intrigued. "What's left for you to do?"

"I'll tell you in a little while," she said.

"Can't I come with you?" he asked. "I've

THE NANCY DREW FILES

always wanted to know what it's like to be a detective and snoop around."

"Philip, please!" Nancy begged him. "There's no time to explain right now. Just wait for me in the parlor."

Philip sighed. "Oh, all right," he said, disappointed. "But you promise to show me what you find?"

"I promise," Nancy said, exasperated. "Now go!"

Philip left her, and Nancy quickly ran upstairs, feeling more and more apprehensive. Nancy now thought she knew whom she was after—and if she was right, the danger was far from over.

She reached the second floor landing and stared down the hallway.

A woman's body was lying on the floor—it was Nila!

Chapter

Sixteen

NILA WASN'T DEAD but was out cold, knocked unconscious apparently by a large brass candlestick that lay on the carpet next to her. On the back of Nila's head, a gigantic lump had already risen.

Nancy could have kicked herself for taking so long getting up there. Thankfully, Nila hadn't been killed outright.

Nancy was now sure she was right. She had been blind—totally blind—but now she could see clearly. All the pieces fit neatly together at last.

She looked down the hall to the door of Eleanor's suite. It was, as Nancy had feared, slightly open. Nancy tiptoed down the hall. As she approached the room, she could hear noises inside—the sound of furniture being dragged around, drawers being opened and searched in the semidarkness.

Nancy edged her way inside. The sitting room was dark, lit only by moonlight, and by the fire in the room's fireplace, which had died down to embers.

The noise was coming from the darkened bedroom. Nancy went silently to the door and stood there, looking inside. It was dark, but the moonlight cast its shadow on the outline of a woman, rifling the drawers of Eleanor's bureau, pulling them out and feeling behind them.

Nancy reached into her jacket pocket, feeling for something. It was there. She pressed a small button, then reached up and flicked on the wall switch.

The woman whirled around. "You," she cried, her eyes narrowed.

"Yes, it's me," Nancy replied evenly. "I'm afraid the game is over—Cecilia."

Cecilia stood by her mother's open dresser drawer. Nancy could see a brown manila envelope in her hand. "Let me guess," Nancy said, gesturing toward the envelope. "The copies of your uncle's new will."

Cecilia shook the hair back out of her face and smiled defiantly. "That's right," she said. "Mother was foolish not to let me destroy them right away. She's always so finicky about right and wrong. She's much too good a person, if you ask me."

"Not too good to help you hide the crimes you've committed," Nancy pointed out.

"I won't let her go to jail for me," Cecilia swore, the wild look in her eyes growing even more intense. "But first things first." Before Nancy could stop her, Cecilia tossed the manila envelope into the fireplace. The dying embers flared, and before Nancy could make a move to rescue the copies of Pierce's new will, they had roared into flame.

"There," Cecilia said with satisfaction, crossing her arms in front of her. "That takes care of that. Now Mother will inherit the money she deserves. And that witch Nila will have to get out of here. I've gotten so tired of living with her, always afraid of what she'll do to us."

"Has she treated you so badly?" Nancy asked.

Cecilia laughed derisively. "I knew what she was up to. She was just waiting until she married Uncle Charles. Then, it would have been the end for the rest of us."

"So you decided to get rid of her," Nancy said, trying to draw Cecilia out.

"Yes," Cecilia replied, a small smile playing on her lips. "I don't mind telling you now. I'll deny it later, of course, and you'll never be able to prove anything. Mother won't turn me in—and she's the only one who knows."

"How are you going to keep your mother from going to jail?" Nancy asked pointedly. "She seems determined to take the blame."

Cecilia's smile vanished. "I'll get her to change her story," she assured Nancy. "She just panicked tonight. She's a very panicky person. Not like me. I'm much smarter than people think I am, you know."

"Yes, you are," Nancy said. "So tell me how you did it. As you say, we're alone, and you can always deny it later."

Cecilia leaned against the dresser, and the little smile returned. "The first thing I did was to doctor that article and make sure Mother found it. I thought she'd show it to Uncle Charles, but I was wrong. She showed it to Karen and Jack instead. I guess she thought they'd have the guts to show it to my uncle, but they didn't. And neither did she. So I had to think of another way to get rid of Nila.

"That's when I wrote that letter, threatening her. But that didn't work either. Nila showed it to Uncle Charles, and he got mad and hired you to come snoop around. I heard someone at the party say that there was a detective there, so I decided to make Nila have an accident. The servants really shouldn't leave rat poison lying around—you never know who's going to swallow it."

She played absentmindedly with a strand of hair. Nancy hoped no one would come into the room—at least not before she'd heard the whole, horrible story.

"Unfortunately, Mother had to come by just then, and she saw me standing over Nila. She took the rat poison away and made me get out of there—and then, I suppose, she switched glasses so no one would find the poison in Nila's glass. I have to hand it to Mother—she's usually wimpy, but that time, she was pretty clever. She sure fooled you, and the doctors never even suspected Nila'd been poisoned.

"On the other hand, Nila never drank enough of her cranberry juice to die, so I knew I'd have to try again. But, first, I had to get you out of the way. As soon as I found out you were the detective Uncle Charles had hired, I started thinking of a way to get rid of you."

"I never even suspected you," Nancy said.

Cecilia's expression grew bitter. "Nobody pays any attention to me," she complained "Their loss."

"I could have died in that car," Nancy said, feeling the anger well up inside her.

"You *should* have died!" Cecilia shot back, her face reddening with fury.

Now it was Nancy's turn to smile. "I guess I'm just too good a driver," she said.

Cecilia ignored the comment. "I took the rag I'd used to wipe off my hands, grabbed Mother's key to Jack and Karen's house, and dumped it in his office waste basket."

"That was you?" Nancy asked. "I thought your mother had dropped it there."

Cecilia shook her head. "Mother would never try to implicate anyone who was innocent," she said. "But I figure Jack deserved whatever he got. And he's so messy, he never throws out his trash, so it was easy."

"Anyway, he wasn't the only one I was making

look guilty. I had everyone thinking Nila was faking it all." She giggled at the thought of it. "But when Uncle Charles made his new will, I knew I had to do something drastic. So I stole the copies. I was going to burn them—but Mother found me first and took the copies away. She locked them here in her room so I couldn't get to them."

Cecilia frowned at the memory of it. "It didn't really matter anyway. I knew that as soon as Uncle Charles knew they were missing, he'd just make a new copy. And even if I got rid of Nila once and for all, he wouldn't leave us his money anymore. He was too angry by that point. That's why I had to kill him."

She looked at Nancy with a frank, open expression as if that explained everything she'd done. Nancy quietly waited for more.

"I sneaked into his room and told him Nila'd sent me up to give him his medicine. Poor Uncle Charles, he never suspected anything. I took the bottle of pills and his water glass to the bathroom, and dissolved six or seven extra pills in the water. I watched him drink it. I'm sure he never even noticed. I thought he'd at least say the water tasted funny.

"Anyway, I knew the police would think Nila had done it. She's the one who was named in the will, and she's the one who always gave him his medicine."

"Your uncle isn't dead," Nancy reminded her.

Cecilia frowned. "No, that's true. But he will

be. Or else he'll be brain damaged. The doctor said so. In either case, he won't be able to tell anyone who gave him the overdose."

"What about the brick that nearly killed Nila?" Nancy asked.

"I wanted her dead, just in case," Cecilia explained. "I mean, Mother still had the copies of the will. I figured she might decide to put them back in Uncle Charle's desk or something stupid like that. She's so honest. Anyway, I rigged the rope with the loop in it so I could yank the brick off the parapet from the second floor window. That was the most clever thing of all, I think. Because even if I missed, I knew everyone would think Nila'd pulled it down herself, just the way she'd faked everything else."

"Brilliant," Nancy said. "I have to admit it. Too bad you didn't apply that wonderful mind of yours to better uses."

Cecilia shrugged. "You can't tell me what to do with my life," she said. "Someday, I'll have a lot of money. And I'll make sure Uncle Charles's foundation has money, too. I like charities. You might say Mother and I have been one of Uncle Charles's charities. But no more. Mother's going to have lots of money, and someday it will all be mine."

"What about Nila?" Nancy asked. "You didn't kill her, you know. She's only unconscious. When she wakes up, she'll tell the police it was you who hit her."

"No, she won't," Cecilia said, shaking her

head and smiling. "She never even saw me. I hit her from behind before she knew I was there. I thought she was going to snoop in Mother's room. She had the keys in her hand. And I had to destroy the will before she got her paws on it."

Cecilia shut the dresser drawer slowly. "And now it's all over," she said, glancing at the ashes in the fireplace. "That was a pretty clever trick you played on Mother, getting her to confess like that. You really didn't know it was her because you couldn't have, could you? I mean, it *wasn't* her—it was me!"

"So it's my word against yours," Nancy said. "And you don't think that's enough?"

"No way," Cecilia said, coming slowly toward Nancy. "And you know it, too. Goodbye, Nancy. Nice try—and better luck next time."

She brushed past Nancy, fluffing her hair as she walked into the darkened sitting room and then out the door into the hallway.

"There's just one thing," Nancy called after her.

Cecilia spun around. "And what is that?" she asked.

Now it was Nancy's turn to smile. Out of her jacket pocket, she pulled her microcassette recorder. "You forgot this," she said.

Cecilia went white. "No," she gasped. "You little sneak!" She lunged for Nancy, knocking the recorder out of her hands. Both girls dove for it, but it skittered out through the door into the hallway.

Nancy was the first to get up and run for the

recorder, but Cecilia was right behind her, and now she had a sharp letter opener in her hand!

Nancy grabbed the recorder and spun around to tackle Cecilia. The two of them fell to the carpet, struggling for the weapon and the recorder.

But just then there was a commotion from the stairs.

"Nancy!" Philip was shouting. He came bounding up the stairs and into the hallway, followed by Karen and Jack. Quickly Nancy disarmed Cecilia and pocketed both the recorder and the letter opener. Before Cecilia could react, Nancy ran over to Philip's side.

He had stopped briefly when he saw Nila, who was just sitting up, rubbing the back of her head and wincing in pain.

"Say, are you all right?" he asked her, bending down next to her.

"I—I think so," Nila said. "Someone hit me on the head."

"With this, I'll bet," Jack said, touching the candlestick with his toe.

Nancy shot Cecilia a look, and Cecilia returned it innocently, blankly, as if their conversation had never even taken place. But Cecilia's eyes were on Nancy's pockets.

"Listen, Nancy," Philip said excitedly. "Listen, Nila—great news! Father's regained consciousness! The doctor said it was a miracle, but it looks like he's going to be all right!"

Cecilia had gone dead white. "No—no brain damage?" she whispered hoarsely.

"Apparently not," Philip said. "Good old Dad—he's a real fighter!"

Nancy was amazed at the sudden gush of filial love coming from Philip Pierce. Karen, too, looked radiantly happy. She and Nila embraced, both of them crying in each others' arms.

"No!" Cecilia cried suddenly. And then she was screaming it, both hands to her head, as she sunk to her knees. "No! NO! NOOOO!"

"Call the police, Philip," Nancy said, looking at the pitiful sight of Cecilia crumbling onto the floor. "Yes, Cecilia, you were right. It *is* all over."

Three months later Nancy and Bess were both honored to be present at the wedding of Charles Pierce and Nila Kirkedottir. Pierce was able to walk down the aisle under his own power— thanks to the heart transplant he'd undergone eight weeks earlier.

Nancy and Bess were late getting there—Bess had had trouble deciding what to wear—and by the time they got to the church, the ceremony had already started. So it wasn't until after the ceremony that Philip caught up to Nancy.

"Hey there, gorgeous!" he called out cheerfully. "Don't I know you?"

"Philip," Nancy said, feeling the usual rush of attraction that hit her whenever he was around. Nancy had successfully avoided Philip ever since the Pierce case was closed. But she didn't pull away now when he kissed her.

"Where've you been hiding?" he asked her as

Bess went off to throw rice at the bride and groom. "I've left messages, but you never return them."

"I just thought it was better if we got a little breathing space between us," Nancy explained. "I mean, I do have a boyfriend."

"Oh, yes, I think you did mention him once," Philip said. "But don't tell me you're going to let a little thing like a boyfriend come between us?"

"It's not such a little thing," Nancy said. "Besides—"

"Don't tell me," he interrupted. "Let me guess. It's because I'm immature and spoiled and don't know how to handle money, right? Well, let me catch you up on the new Philip Pierce. I've opened a savings account, and I contribute to it regularly out of my salary at Dad's company. I even make monthly contributions to the Pierce Foundation. At night I'm going for a degree in business. I'm having no fun at all, because I work like a dog and spend zero money on going out— but I've actually been happy, believe it or not."

"That's great, Philip!" Nancy said, sincerely glad for him. "So you and your dad are getting along?"

"Fantastically," he told her. "I'm amazed myself about it. But Dad's different now—he's got a new heart, a new wife, and a new lease on life. His whole attitude's changed. He's taken over the company and the foundation personally again. He's up at six every day and works like a dog. But now that I work with him, I'm coming to appreciate the side of Dad I always missed growing up. I kind of like the guy, to tell you the truth."

"Oh, Philip, I'm so happy to hear all this," Nancy said. "How are Karen and Jack doing?"

"Great!" he told her. "Jack's in a gamblers' support group, and he and Karen are in couple counseling. They seem to be making progress, and Jack's working hard, for a change. I know because I'm his boss now." He winked at Nancy mischievously. "Tom's betting parlor closed down, and Tom's getting out of prison next month after doing ninety days. But I guess all's well that end's well, huh?"

"What about Eleanor?" Nancy asked.

Philip sighed. "She's bearing up," he said. "She got a suspended sentence for being an accessory. But she's all broken up about Cecilia, I'm afraid.

"It's sad about Cecilia, of course," he went on. "We're all crushed about it. Let's just hope she can make a fresh start when she gets out of prison. After all, if I can improve, there's hope for all of us."

Nancy gave his arm a squeeze. "That's why I like you," she told him. "It's your sunny, optimistic nature."

"Ah, so that's it!" he said, arching his eyebrows. "I thought it was my smashing good looks."

The bride and groom drove off in their silver Rolls-Royce, while the crowd waved and cheered. "Nila sure looked beautiful," Nancy commented.

"She certainly did," he agreed. "She's a fantastic woman, you know? I never appreciated her before. I guess I felt too threatened by her. But now that Dad's remade his will—and we're all in it equally—everyone's made peace. We've even become friends, to tell you the truth. Nila's running the foundation with Dad, and she's got big plans for it. In fact, you'll probably be invited to the big benefit bash."

"Me?" Nancy asked, surprised. "Why?"

"Oh, they're going to have all the local celebrities," Philip told her, smiling. "And, of course, that includes the greatest detective ever to hit River Heights!"

Nancy's next case:

It's Fashion Week at the River Heights mall, and Bess is in heaven. She's working at Wicked, the hottest boutique in town, and she's about to make her modeling debut—with rock singer Lynxette! But someone is shoplifting designer jackets from the store, and if it keeps up, the fashion show will be a total bust. For Nancy, tracking down the thief could prove both delicate and dangerous. Bess has fallen for one of the top suspects, and cracking the case could break her heart. But the shoplifter is turning more brazen by the day, and Nancy knows that the culprit will do anything to get the jackets . . . no matter who gets hurt in the process . . . in *Wicked Ways*, Case #113 in The Nancy Drew Files™.

THE HARDY BOYS CASEFILES

☐ #1: DEAD ON TARGET	73992-1/$3.99		☐ #72: SCREAMERS	73108-4/$3.75
☐ #2: EVIL, INC.	73668-X/$3.75		☐ #73: BAD RAP	73109-2/$3.99
☐ #3: CULT OF CRIME	68726-3/$3.99		☐ #74: ROAD PIRATES	73110-6/$3.99
☐ #4: THE LAZARUS PLOT	73995-6/$3.75		☐ #75: NO WAY OUT	73111-4/$3.99
☐ #5: EDGE OF DESTRUCTION	73669-8/$3.99		☐ #76: TAGGED FOR TERROR	73112-2/$3.99
☐ #6: THE CROWNING OF TERROR	73670-1/$3.50		☐ #77: SURVIVAL RUN	79461-2/$3.99
☐ #7: DEATHGAME	73672-8/$3.99		☐ #78: THE PACIFIC CONSPIRACY	79462-0/$3.99
☐ #8: SEE NO EVIL	73673-6/$3.50		☐ #79: DANGER UNLIMITED	79463-9/$3.99
☐ #9: THE GENIUS THIEVES	73674-4/$3.50		☐ #80: DEAD OF NIGHT	79464-7/$3.99
☐ #12: PERFECT GETAWAY	73675-2/$3.50		☐ #81: SHEER TERROR	79465-5/$3.99
☐ #14: TOO MANY TRAITORS	73677-9/$3.50		☐ #82: POISONED PARADISE	79466-3/$3.99
☐ #32: BLOOD MONEY	74665-0/$3.50		☐ #83: TOXIC REVENGE	79467-1/$3.99
☐ #35: THE DEAD SEASON	74105-5/$3.50		☐ #84: FALSE ALARM	79468-X/$3.99
☐ #41: HIGHWAY ROBBERY	70038-3/$3.75		☐ #85: WINNER TAKE ALL	79469-8/$3.99
☐ #44: CASTLE FEAR	74615-4/$3.75		☐ #86: VIRTUAL VILLAINY	79470-1/$3.99
☐ #45: IN SELF-DEFENSE	70042-1/$3.75		☐ #87: DEAD MAN IN DEADWOOD	79471-X/$3.99
☐ #47: FLIGHT INTO DANGER	70044-8/$3.75		☐ #88: INFERNO OF FEAR	79472-8/$3.99
☐ #49: DIRTY DEEDS	70046-4/$3.99		☐ #89: DARKNESS FALLS	79473-6/$3.99
☐ #50: POWER PLAY	70047-2/$3.99		☐ #90: DEADLY ENGAGEMENT	79474-4/$3.99
☐ #53: WEB OF HORROR	73089-4/$3.99		☐ #91: HOT WHEELS	79475-2/$3.99
☐ #54: DEEP TROUBLE	73090-8/$3.99		☐ #92: SABOTAGE AT SEA	79476-0/$3.99
☐ #55: BEYOND THE LAW	73091-6/$3.50		☐ #93: MISSION: MAYHEM	88204-X/$3.99
☐ #56: HEIGHT OF DANGER	73092-4/$3.99		☐ #94: A TASTE FOR TERROR	88205-8/$3.99
☐ #57: TERROR ON TRACK	73093-2/$3.99		☐ #95: ILLEGAL PROCEDURE	88206-6/$3.99
☐ #60: DEADFALL	73096-7/$3.99		☐ #96: AGAINST ALL ODDS	88207-4/$3.99
☐ #61: GRAVE DANGER	73097-5/$3.99		☐ #97: PURE EVIL	88208-2/$3.99
☐ #62: FINAL GAMBIT	73098-3/$3.75		☐ #98: MURDER BY MAGIC	88209-0/$3.99
☐ #63: COLD SWEAT	73099-1/$3.75		☐ #99: FRAME-UP	88210-4/$3.99
☐ #64: ENDANGERED SPECIES	73100-9/$3.99		☐ #100: TRUE THRILLER	88211-2/$3.99
☐ #65: NO MERCY	73101-7/$3.99		☐ #101: PEAK OF DANGER	88212-0/$3.99
☐ #66: THE PHOENIX EQUATION	73102-5/$3.99		☐ #102: WRONG SIDE OF THE LAW	88213-9/$3.99
☐ #68: ROUGH RIDING	73104-1/$3.75		☐ #103: CAMPAIGN OF CRIME	88214-7/$3.99
☐ #69: MAYHEM IN MOTION	73105-X/$3.75		☐ #104: WILD WHEELS	88215-5/$3.99
☐ #71: REAL HORROR	73107-6/$3.99		☐ #105: LAW OF THE JUNGLE	50428-2/$3.99
			☐ #106: SHOCK JOCK	50429-0/$3.99

Simon & Schuster Mail Order
200 Old Tappan Rd., Old Tappan, N.J. 07675

Please send me the books I have checked above. I am enclosing $_____ (please add $0.75 to cover the postage and handling for each order. Please add appropriate sales tax). Send check or money order--no cash or C.O.D.'s please. Allow up to six weeks for delivery. For purchase over $10.00 you may use VISA: card number, expiration date and customer signature must be included.

Name _____

Address _____

City _____ State/Zip _____

VISA Card # _____ Exp. Date _____

Signature _____ 762-29

By Carolyn Keene

Nancy Drew is going to college.
For Nancy, it's a time of change....A change
of address....A change of heart.

Nancy Drew on Campus™#1:
❑ New Lives, New Loves......52737-1/$3.99

Nancy Drew on Campus™#2:
❑ On Her Own......................52741-X/$3.99

Nancy Drew on Campus™#3:
❑ Don't Look Back................52744-4/$3.99

Nancy Drew on Campus™#4:
❑ Tell Me The Truth.............52745-2/$3.99

Archway Paperback
Published by Pocket Books